EXECUTION FILE

EXECUTION FILE

THE SILENCER SERIES
BOOK 19

MIKE RYAN

WWW.MIKERYANBOOKS.COM

ALSO BY MIKE RYAN

For my Family

Thank you Liz, Brianna, Jake, Matthew, and Michael for your help on deciding on a title for this book.

1

Recker and Haley walked into the office, already tired out by the events of the morning. It was one of their more hectic ones. They'd already snuffed out a kidnapping attempt, and a convenience store robbery. And it wasn't even noon yet.

"You ever get the feeling sometimes that this city's going down the tubes?" Haley asked.

"Just another day," Recker replied. "What's the song... Mama Told Me There'd Be Days Like These? It's one of those days."

Haley took a deep breath and looked at his watch. "I'm already tired out and it's not even lunchtime yet. Speaking of which, maybe we should go out and get some while we still have the time. Assuming we do now."

Recker looked at their other partner, who was busy

stroking the keys of his computer. Jones peered up at them, overhearing their conversation.

"Are you awaiting an answer from me?"

Recker shrugged. "Guess it depends if you wanna give one."

"We have nothing else on the docket today from what I can see."

"We should head out now, then, while we have the chance," Haley said.

Recker seemed agreeable. "You wanna join us?"

Jones briefly stopped typing, considering the offer. "No, I don't think I will."

"C'mon, David, you can't stay in this office all day," Haley said. "You said yourself that nothing's on the table."

"That I can see. As you can tell by the morning, and like Michael said, this appears to be one of those days."

"I know you can rig something up to get an alert on your phone while you're out," Recker said.

"I can, but... I'll just sit this one out," Jones replied. "Next time."

"We're gonna hold you to that," Haley said.

Recker and Haley weren't going to continue badgering him about it, though they both believed that Jones needed to get out and stretch his legs a little more. As Recker and Haley left the office and went to their car, they discussed where to go.

"How about one of those small outdoor cafes or

something?" Haley asked. "I don't feel like sitting inside."

"Yeah, I'll go along with that."

"Wanna see if Mia wants to join us?"

"I can do that," Recker said, pulling out his phone as he got in the driver's seat. He instantly dialed Mia's number.

She picked up right away. "What's wrong?"

Recker laughed. "Nothing's wrong. Why do you automatically assume something's wrong?"

"Because it's... not even noon yet. And you're calling."

"Nothing's wrong. I promise."

"You're sure you're not just buttering me up for the moment just to drop a bomb on me later?"

"You're not being set up."

"OK. Then what are you calling for?"

"We just finished a couple things, and we were going to lunch. Just wanted to see if you wanted to join us?"

"Who's we?" Mia asked.

"Chris. Me. You."

"Awe, that's so sweet. You wanted to have lunch with me."

"Well it was really Chris' idea."

"Thanks a lot!"

Recker kept laughing. "But I guess I could look at you again. You know, if I'm forced to."

"Oh, if you're forced to? Laying it on pretty thick today, huh?"

"I guess you're not that bad to look at."

Mia finally let out a laugh, too. "What couch do you want to be sleeping on later?"

"Whatever one you're on too."

"Well I'm not sure if that's happening now."

"You know I'm just teasing."

"I know. And I wish I could join you guys for lunch. But I can't."

"Why not?" Recker asked. "I thought you were off today."

"Well, I was. But, since you were out and working, I figured I may as well, too. Someone called out, and they asked if I could come in, so... since I didn't think I was doing anything, I said yes."

"Oh. When are you going in?"

"I'm leaving in about twenty minutes. So I won't be home until tonight."

"OK, well, try not to get into any trouble."

"Oh, you're telling me that?" Mia said. "I should be saying that about you."

"You know I never get into any trouble."

"Ha! That's a good one. Trying comedy, these days?"

"Stretching my talents," Recker answered.

"That's really stretching. By a lot."

"Yeah, probably so."

"I'll see you later, OK? Love you."

4

"Love you too."

"And I love you too!" Haley yelled.

Mia heard him. "Ditto, Chris!"

Recker hung up and put his phone back in his pocket.

"She's not coming?" Haley asked.

Recker shook his head. "She's about to go in to work. Won't be home till later."

"Thought she had off?"

"Someone called out."

"Guess it's just us, then."

"Yeah, looks that way."

"Maybe there's something wrong with us," Haley said.

"How you figure?"

"Well, first David turned us down, now Mia. Maybe we're not that fun to hang out with."

Recker smiled. "Well, neither one of us is known for our outgoing personalities and bubbly behavior."

"Maybe we should try acting more perky."

"I'll let you work on that one."

They then drove to a small restaurant that they'd been to before. It had a few tables outside for customers to sit. It was a nice enough day with the weather. Once they parked, they got out of their vehicle and started walking to the restaurant. It was a normal day in the area. Lots of cars passing, people walking on the sidewalks, a good amount of activity.

As Recker and Haley were about to enter the building, Recker glanced across the street. There was nothing that jumped out at him. It was just a reflex action. He noticed several men getting out of expensive-looking black cars. The premium vehicles that wealthy people usually drove in.

Recker stopped for a moment to keep looking at them, with his partner not even realizing he was now walking alone. Haley continued on to the restaurant. Recker wasn't sure why he was so intrigued by what he was looking at. He just knew that he was.

There were four men that for some reason grabbed Recker's attention. He could only see the back of their bodies, but something was drawing his gaze. He continued staring at them, though he couldn't say why if he was asked. The men were all dressed in nice-looking suits. The kind that weren't bought off the rack in your favorite discount department store. These were tailored.

The four men all walked over to the office building. The ten-floor building was mostly glass, with big windows that encompassed the entire front facade. Once the men reached the front door, one of the men pulled open the door to let the others in first. As the men walked in, the remaining man instinctively looked across the street. It seemed as if he and Recker locked eyes. The man tilted his head, the way one does when you're not exactly sure if you're seeing correctly. It was almost as if he recognized Recker's face.

But it was a face that Recker knew as well. At least

he thought he did. As Recker continued his stare, the man put his head down and wiped his nose, almost as if he were embarrassed at being spotted. He quickly went inside the building.

Recker took a few steps toward the street. He wasn't ready to dart across the street yet or anything, but he did seem to be getting drawn that way. His concentration wasn't broken until he felt Haley's hand grab his arm. Recker spun his head toward his partner, almost surprised that he was there.

"You OK?"

Recker only looked at him for a second, before putting his eyes on the building across the street again. He wasn't sure what was going on here. Maybe it was all an illusion.

"Mike? You all right?"

"Uh, yeah. Yeah, I guess so."

"What's wrong? Looks like you saw a ghost or something?"

Recker turned toward his partner again. "I think maybe I did."

2

Both Recker and Haley stayed in place for a minute. Neither seemed quite sure what to do next. They were both kind of in shock.

"You wanna say that again?" Haley asked.

Recker started shaking his head. He couldn't explain it. Hell, maybe he was hallucinating for all he knew. They had been working pretty much every day for the last couple of weeks. Maybe all the extra activity was catching up to them. Maybe that was it. It had to be. There really couldn't be any other reason.

But yet, there he was, standing there, his head in a fog, sure that what he saw really was there. His vision seemed normal. He didn't have a headache. The weather was clear. He couldn't have been seeing things.

"Mike, you all right?"

Recker took a deep breath. "I guess so."

"What the hell is going on? You were fine five minutes ago. Now all of a sudden you're looking like you just escaped a horror movie."

Recker opened his mouth, but no words came out. He pointed to the large office building across the street.

"I just, uh, saw people going into that building there."

"Yeah? And? Something wrong with that?"

Recker took another deep breath. "It's… the one guy I saw… I almost thought I recognized him."

"Oh? Friend of yours?"

"Nope."

"Then what's the issue?"

Recker hesitated before he answered. "I killed him."

Haley snapped his head back, not quite prepared to hear those words. "You what?"

"I killed him. A couple years before I came here and met David."

Haley looked at his partner like he had suddenly gone crazy. It might not have been too far from the truth if he really believed what he was saying.

"So you're saying you just saw a guy go in that building… that you killed a few years back?"

Recker nodded. "That's what I'm saying. Pretty crazy, right?"

"Unbelievable, almost." Haley looked up at the sky. "Look, the sun's out, it's pretty hot, it's glaring down, maybe it created an angle where you kinda just thought you noticed someone who looked like this guy."

Recker glanced up at the sky, as well. A hot sun has been known to play a trick on people from time to time. "Yeah. Maybe." He didn't think that was it, though. Not this time.

"It's obviously not the same guy, Mike. If you killed this guy, which I assume you'd know if you did, he obviously couldn't still be standing here, could he?"

"Not likely."

"Unless there's some new scientific marvel that I haven't heard about recently."

"Seems pretty unlikely, huh?" Recker replied.

"I'd say it was. So there you go," Haley said. "Obviously the sun's playing tricks on you. It's physically impossible to be the same guy."

"Unless I didn't kill him."

"Wait a minute, you said you did."

"I thought I did."

"Aren't you sure?"

"Thought I was."

He playfully tapped Recker on the arm. Recker let out a smile, but he still wasn't sure. Haley could see that his friend was still bothered by what he thought he saw.

"I tell you what. If this has really got you spooked, there's an easy solution to figuring this out."

"What's that?" Recker asked.

"Let's just walk over to that building, go inside, and

ask if we could see the people that just went in there. You can get a better look at their faces. Then you'll be able to see that it wasn't the same guy. Maybe someone who's just a look-alike. Then you won't have to worry about it anymore." Haley rubbed his stomach. "Then we can get something to eat."

"And say what when we get in there?"

Haley shrugged. He didn't seem worried about it. "We'll figure it out when we get there. Thought we saw an old friend, a colleague, some classmates from college? Something along those lines. We always figure it out."

Recker seemed agreeable to that. "OK. Let's go."

The two men waited at the curb for a few cars to pass, then scurried across the street. Once they got to the office building door, Recker paused for a second. Haley could tell a lot of thoughts were going through his friend's mind. He actually couldn't recall ever seeing him so unnerved before. It was clear Recker thought he saw something. Something that freaked him out. Now it was just a question of whether he was right. But they were about to find out.

Haley threw open the door and the two men walked in. It was a good-sized lobby, with one desk in the middle of the room, belonging to a receptionist. She greeted them with a smile as they approached her desk.

"Can I help you?"

Haley spoke up. "Yes, we just wanted to talk to the

men that just came in here. They looked like old college pals of ours. Haven't seen them in some time."

"I'm afraid nobody's come in here."

"I just saw four men come in here," Recker said. "Expensive suits, sunglasses, tight haircuts. In the last ten minutes."

"I'm sorry. Nobody's walked in since Mrs. Winningham this morning. That was two hours ago."

"Have you been away from your desk at all?"

"No, I'm afraid not."

Recker looked at his partner. "I know what I saw."

"Are you sure nobody's been in here?" Haley asked.

"I've been sitting here," the receptionist answered. "I haven't seen anyone."

"Four men?"

"I'm sorry, no."

"Maybe you went to get coffee or something?"

The woman continued shaking her head. She was sticking with the same story. "Nope. No one."

"What businesses operate here?" Recker asked.

The woman pointed to a black sign on the wall. It was the kind that had the glass on the outside, and white lettering on the inside with the names of the businesses, along with their unit numbers. Recker and Haley walked over to it.

"Stand between me and her," Recker whispered.

Haley blocked the woman's view as Recker took out his phone and quickly took a picture of the businesses that were listed. He then put the phone back in his pocket. He was skeptical about the woman. He knew she was lying. He knew it. He didn't imagine the men walking in there. Maybe he was looking at a different guy than the one who was supposed to be dead, but he didn't make up four people and a car out front. That much was clear.

"What do you wanna do?" Haley asked.

"I dunno. This woman's not gonna tell us anything. And I don't want to push it right now."

As they looked at the business directory, nothing jumped out at them as unusual or set off any alarms. But something was obviously not what it seemed.

"Is there anything else I can help you with?" the woman asked.

They turned back to her.

"No," Recker said. "Sorry. I must have been mistaken."

She had a smile on her face. "Oh, no problem. It happens."

Recker and Haley walked out of the building, stopping once they hit the sidewalk out in front. They looked up at the building, almost expecting someone to be looking down at them from a window. Haley could see his partner was still worked up about this.

"Hey, let's go over and eat, and figure out our next steps."

Recker agreed. "I'm not crazy. Maybe the one guy isn't who I think he is, but I didn't dream up four of them."

"I know you didn't. I got the feeling that recep-tionist was keeping something from us."

"Like four people who just walked in?"

"Yeah. The question is what are they hiding?"

The two walked across the street and finally made it to the restaurant, taking up a seat at one of the outdoor tables. They still had a view of the building across from them, so if the men came back out, they'd clearly see it. Of course, Recker had his doubts about that. He knew the one man obviously saw him. And if they knew Recker came into the building to check on him, and that they were sitting across the street, it was unlikely they'd just come waltzing out the front door. There was likely a back door with their name on it.

After they ordered, Haley started quizzing his partner on what he thought he saw.

"You wanna explain how you can see a guy that you thought was dead?"

Recker took a few seconds to clear his head, and get everything straight in his mind. It'd been well over seven or eight years, by that point.

"I was on an assignment for the agency. You know the ones. Execution file. Simple takeout mission. Do the job, lay low for a couple days, then extract yourself through the usual channels."

"Who was the target?" Haley asked.

"Marko Petrović. Real bad guy. He was a Croatian jack-of-all-trades type of guy. Most of what he hooked up with, though, was violent. Bodyguard, assassin, mercenary, mostly involving drugs, money, and guns. He was also heavily into the trafficking business. Again, money, drugs, and people. Just a real bad guy all the way around."

"Hired himself out?"

"To the highest bidder. Every time. And he didn't care who he had to hurt to accomplish the task of whatever he was hired for."

"So you were sent to take him out?"

Recker nodded. "And I thought I did. Until today."

"How does that happen, though? I know you're not sloppy. You wouldn't have done a half-ass job out there."

"I took him out from a distance. Sniper rifle." Recker's mind immediately immersed himself back into that day, like he'd never left it. "It was a crowded street. Some type of market going on, or a festival, or something. I hit him. He went down. I know I hit him. Got him in the chest."

"Maybe it wasn't a fatal blow."

"I never got to check on him. As you can imagine, it got pretty crazy around there after the shot. But I know I drilled him. Anyway, word came down the following day that his body was in the morgue."

"Did you check it?"

"Not me. The agency didn't want to risk sending me in for that in case the people Petrović was working for were around and watching."

"How'd they verify, then?"

"Apparently they had a police contact who went to the morgue, then verified it was Petrović that was lying there. Then the agency closed the books on it. I was assigned to a new case, and that was it."

"All neat and tidy," Haley said. "What do you know about that police contact?"

"Nothing. Wasn't my contact. The agency said they had it covered. Wasn't my concern anymore."

"So you think Petrović wasn't really killed? That maybe this police officer was on the take, paid to say Petrović was dead, then everyone went on about their business like nothing ever happened?"

"I don't know. Never thought anything of it until now."

"Never any chatter about Petrović still being out there?"

Recker shook his head. "Nothing that I ever heard. And a guy like that, I'd think his name would pop up again within the last six or seven years."

"How would he recognize you, though? You said you locked eyes with the guy over there and you thought he recognized you."

"Well, before that fatal shot in the street, we had a couple of other close encounters. You know I always preferred to get closer to my targets. We engaged in three other confrontations before that. Neither of us were able to get the upper hand. Finally resorted to that sniper shot."

"So he would definitely know you again if he saw you. Assuming he's still alive."

"I don't think there's any doubt."

"And he looked the same?"

"Not quite," Recker answered. "He used to have long hair, down to his shoulders. The guy across the street looked like his head was closely shaved. And he had a hat on. But his face… I'd never forget that face."

"So how do you wanna handle this?"

"Handle what?"

"Well we gotta figure out what's going on here, don't we?"

"What if I'm just hallucinating or something?"

"You're not. I don't know whether you saw Petrović or not, but there's obviously something going on in that building. That receptionist gave off bad vibes, and even if it's not Petrović, I know you didn't dream up four people going in there. So there's something."

"Is it something we wanna intrude upon, though?"

"I'd say yes," Haley said. "Because in the event that it actually is Petrović, that means you've got unfinished business. And something big is going on here. Not to mention it'd bring up a host of other questions."

"Like how a dead man can still be walking the streets?"

"That too. But if Petrović was an execution file, they always get finished. Always."

3
─────

Recker and Haley remained seated at their table, long after they had finished their lunch. Luckily, nobody else was itching for a table yet. They ordered a couple other drinks, non-alcoholic, while they waited. They hadn't seen anyone else go in or out of that building, though.

"Pretty strange," Haley said.

"Which part?"

"Well, all of it. But I'm mostly referring to the fact that we've been sitting here for two hours and haven't seen a single person enter or leave that building. Kind of weird. Ten-floor building, dozens of businesses, and nobody's gone in or out."

No sooner had the words left his lips, then they saw a couple people walk in. Looked like a regular couple. Nothing unusual about them.

"Figures," Haley said. "Make a liar out of me."

They thought they might have had something with the lack of activity, but their ideas were soon blown apart, as suddenly dozens of people started walking in.

"Maybe everyone was at lunch."

After a few more minutes, Recker finally got up.

"What are you doing?"

"We're just wasting our time here," Recker said. "Our guys aren't coming out."

"Yeah, you're probably right."

"And we're not gonna learn anything by just sitting here."

They walked back across the street, but instead of going inside the building again, walked around the block until they came up to the rear of the building. There were a couple of cars parked there, though none were the ones Recker saw the four men getting out of.

"Well, the back door looks like the exit," Haley said.

"Yeah. Let's head back to the office and start running these things down."

"Give David a heads-up?"

"Uh, not yet. First, I wanna make a call. You drive on the way back."

They went back to their car and headed for the office. Along the way, Recker called Michelle Lawson.

"Hey, I was just thinking about you," Lawson said.

"Oh?"

She laughed. "Don't get worried. I was just thinking that I hadn't heard from you in a while."

"Oh. Well, glad I could put that to rest now."

"I'm assuming you're not just calling to say hi."

"Uh, hi."

Lawson laughed harder. "You're not good at small-talk. I know something's on your mind. It's fine. Just come out with it."

"What do you know about a man named Marko Petrović?"

Lawson was silent for a moment, thinking it over. "Never heard of him. Why?"

"Don't recognize the name?"

"No, should I?"

"He's a... a guy from my past."

"Oh. Well that sounds ominous. A guy from your past. Mysterious. And creepy."

"He's also supposed to be dead."

"Oh. Well then what's the problem? Why are you asking about him?"

Recker sighed. "Because I thought I saw him today."

Lawson was quiet again. "I'm sorry, what?"

"You heard right. I thought I saw him."

"I... I don't even know how to respond to that. He's dead. But you saw him?"

"That's right?"

"Um... do you need a vacation or something? Or the name of a therapist? I've got a few in mind."

"I don't need a doctor. What I need are some answers."

"I'm not sure I can give you any."

"You can poke around," Recker said.

"Into what?"

"My files. You might be the only one who can."

"What am I poking around for?"

"Marko Petrović."

"The dead guy," Lawson said.

"Yeah."

"And why are we so interested in someone who's no longer with us? Or, supposedly not, or… I'm confusing myself."

"Like I said, I'm not that sure that he's not."

Lawson loudly sighed into the phone. She was obviously not following along. "And he's dead. Except he's not."

"Look, I know it sounds crazy."

Lawson let out a laugh. "You know what? It's probably not even the craziest thing I've heard today, if you can believe that. But you know, you do have an extensive file from your time here. I'm not even up to date on all of it."

"It was five, six, seven years ago. Somewhere around there. Croatia."

"Marko Petrović? He's dead, but you saw him."

"Listen, I can't explain how or why I saw him. All I know is that I killed him some time ago, at least I thought I did, but now I think I saw him."

"Where?"

"Going into some office building."

"In Philly?"

"Yeah."

Recker could imagine the looks he was getting on the other side of the phone. He wouldn't have blamed anyone for thinking he was going nuts. It sounded crazy just talking about it.

"Look, I shot the guy. Thought he was dead. A day later, someone visited the morgue and confirmed he was DOA. I didn't provide the visual confirmation."

"Oh, now I get it. You think maybe someone did some questionable work there."

"I don't know."

"Well the file's not going to confirm anything other than him being dead," Lawson said.

"But maybe it'll provide some other names that would give some indication as to why he might be alive."

"And you're positive you saw him?"

"A hundred percent? No. But I believe it was him."

"OK, but, I'm still not sure I'm not going to be able to give you many answers."

"Maybe not," Recker said. "But maybe the file says something different from what I was told."

"Oh. I see what you're saying. But if they didn't really want him dead, why would they send you to kill him in the first place?"

Recker didn't have an answer for that one. "I don't know. Doesn't really make much sense."

"Maybe he's got a doppelgänger."

"Always possible, I guess."

"All right, I can see that this is a big thing for you, so I'll start running it down and see what I can come up with."

"I appreciate it."

"I guess the question has to be asked. Depending on what I find out... how much truth do you want?"

"All of it. Don't hold anything back."

"No matter how much of a rabbit hole it might go down?"

"I just wanna know if I have an unfinished job or not."

"OK. Will do. I'll call you later. Can't guarantee a time, though."

"I understand. Whenever you can."

By the time Recker and Haley got back to the office, they found Jones in the exact same spot as when they left. At the computer.

"You ever move from there?" Recker asked.

Jones didn't respond. He only gave him a look. He took his eyes off his partner for a second to return to his work, but noticed Recker walked past him on the way to the couch. Recker sighed as he plopped himself down. Jones continued with his work, but only for a second, as he peered over at his friend again. Recker kept moving his head around, looking at the wall, or the ceiling. It was clear he had something on his mind. Something heavy.

"Did you two have a good lunch?" Jones asked.

"Oh yeah," Haley answered.

Jones continued looking at Recker, who clearly had something bothering him. It looked like his mind was elsewhere.

"Anything else on the docket yet?" Haley asked.

"Not as of yet. Why? Are you bored already?"

"Not me."

Jones glanced at Recker again, then back at Haley. He motioned towards Recker, wondering what the issue was with him. Haley just shrugged, not wanting to be the one to explain it.

"Michael. Why don't you say what's on your mind?"

Recker just stared at him for a moment. He then got up and reached into his pocket, before walking over to the desk. He tossed down a piece of paper with a name on it. Jones picked it up.

"Marko Petrović," Jones read. "Who is he?"

A look of anguish came over Recker's face, as if he didn't really want to say again. "Can you just run him down? See what you come up with."

"You're bringing us jobs now? As if we don't have enough to do?"

"I just... wanna see if you can dig up any traces of him over the last several years?"

Jones raised an eyebrow. "Several years? Traces?" He glanced at Haley for a second, before turning his attention back to Recker. It sounded like there was more to the story. "What exactly are we talking about here?"

"Well, I guess you should buckle in."

Recker went back over to the couch and sat down again. Jones wasn't sure where this was going. Recker then relayed their morning, and early afternoon, making sure he didn't miss a beat. Everything was there. From the moment they walked out of that office, to the moment he put eyes on the man he thought was Petrović, to calling Lawson, and back to the second they walked in again.

"So that's it," Recker said. "That's everything."

Jones leaned back in his chair. He looked a little stunned. "Well. That certainly isn't the normal, is it? It appears as if maybe I should have gone to lunch with you two, after all, doesn't it?"

"I told you you needed to get out more. See what happens when you stay here?"

"And you're sure it's the same guy?"

Recker was getting tired of hearing the same question, but he knew it was understandable considering the circumstances. He'd probably ask it, too, if he was in the other chair.

"All I can say is what I think I saw," Recker said. "The what's, the why's, the how's… I don't know any of that. All I know is what I saw."

Jones started moving his head as he looked at his friend. "OK. I guess we should get started, then."

"OK." Recker moved around the desk and sat in a chair. "While you're doing that, I'm gonna start looking into these businesses. Maybe one of them is not as legit as they appear to be."

"I'll give you a hand," Haley said.

Recker put his phone down on the desk, between his and Haley's computers. Recker would take care of the left half of the list, while Haley would take the right. Between the three of them, they hoped they'd find something of interest. Or at least something that would dispel the notion altogether.

Recker was sure of one thing, though. If Marko Petrović really was still alive, there'd be a trace of him somewhere. He was sure of that. The Petrović he knew wasn't the type who could disappear completely for years on end. Petrović left a trail everywhere he'd ever been. Usually dead bodies. So if it really was Petrović that Recker locked eyes with on that street, there'd be a trail somewhere. Maybe it was only bread crumbs. But it'd be there. They just had to find it.

4

The night wore on, and while they thankfully didn't have any other business pop up, they also never got any closer to finding that first bread crumb they hoped would pop up. Once midnight hit, they called it a night and went home. Well, Recker went home. Jones and Haley stayed in the office, still working, taking turns napping on the couch during the night. Recker probably would have stayed with them if he were still a single man.

Once Recker got home, Mia was waiting for him with a kiss as he walked in. There was tension in his lips. She could feel it. Along with his embrace, she could tell something was wrong.

"So what is it?"

"What's what?" Recker replied.

"The problem."

"There's no problem."

She took his hand and led him over to the couch, where they both sat down. She held his hand.

"Don't give me that. I know better. And no secrets. Remember?"

"Shows that much, huh?"

Mia smiled. "Yeah. And I've just become pretty good at reading you."

Recker took a deep breath while he rubbed his chin. Once again, he relayed the entire story from beginning to end.

"So that's it, huh?" Mia asked.

"That's it. Pretty crazy, right?"

"Yeah. I'd say so. So what else is bothering you?"

"What else? Isn't that enough?"

"There's more. I can see it."

Recker rubbed his face as he took another deep breath. "I guess it's... maybe I'm just starting to doubt myself now."

"Doubt yourself? Why?"

"Seeing ghosts. Up until this morning, I thought Petrović was dead. Maybe he still is. Maybe I really am seeing things."

"You're not."

Recker looked a little more distraught than usual. With Mia, he could let his guard down a little more. With the others, even though Jones and Haley were his friends, he didn't want to show any signs of weakness. He had to be strong. Confident. He always knew. Even if he really didn't.

But with Mia, he didn't have to always be right. He could show the things that he feared. This was one of those times.

"What if this is like the dreams?"

Mia looked confused. "What does one have to do with the other?"

"What if this is just like a continuation of that? The dreams were a result of everything I'd been through. And everything I feared might happen because of that."

"I'm still not sure what they've got to do with each other."

"What if I'm just seeing things that aren't really there? All the jobs, all the missions, all the faces... what if I'm just losing it? Here's a guy that I know I shot. He should be dead. What if everything's been building up inside for all these years, and now I'm losing touch with reality?"

Mia squeezed him tightly. "You're not. Just so you know, I believe you."

"I'm not sure anybody else does."

"What? You said you guys spent all night looking for this guy."

"Yeah. And we found nothing," Recker said. "I'm not sure if they were looking because they really believed my story, or because they just didn't want to admit that I sounded like a nutjob."

"Mike, they do not think that."

"How could they not? I'm starting to think that. We

29

didn't find one trace of Petrović in the last five years. Nothing. How can a guy like that just disappear?"

Mia didn't have any answers on that front. She did know that she trusted Recker more than anything. If he thought he saw something, she didn't question it. She believed it. She just had to make him believe it too.

"It's not like you to question yourself. You're usually more confident about things."

"When I saw him, I thought I was," Recker replied. "I really believed it. But all that time we spent in the office looking for him... we didn't find anything."

"That doesn't mean nothing's there. It just means that you didn't find it yet."

"Maybe there's nothing to find. Maybe the guy's really dead. And maybe I'm finally starting to crack."

"Don't say that. You're not. I think I'd see signs if you were losing it."

"Sometimes the people closest to you are the ones that see the least."

"You're saying I don't want to see it, therefore I don't?"

"Something like that."

"I didn't ignore the dreams," Mia said. "And I encouraged you to get help for it."

"Well, it's tough to ignore someone who's kicking and screaming and waking you up every night."

"Mike, you are not losing your mind. If you think you saw this guy, then you saw him. I have absolutely no doubts about that."

"Wish I didn't."

"Didn't what?"

"Have doubts. We checked passports, ID's, driver's licenses, credit cards, known family members, everything you can think of that might belong to him. Everything. Didn't find a single thing that could be linked back to him."

"You just started. You have to give it time."

"Petrović is a violent, dangerous man. People like him don't slip away quietly never to be heard from again. I know his history. His background. He's not capable of doing nothing for the last six years."

"So maybe he didn't. Maybe he was doing all of those things that he used to do under a different name. I mean, he'd have to, right? Otherwise, what good would faking his death do?"

"But we checked for aliases," Recker said. "Nothing came up."

"Like I said, it just means you didn't find it yet. If he did all those things you say, and he's supposed to be dead, he's obviously going to make it difficult to find him again."

"You'd think a security camera would pick him up somewhere in the world and set off an alert, though."

"Maybe he had some plastic surgery to alter his appearance?"

Recker shook his head. "The face I looked at appeared to be the same."

The two were quiet for a few moments, though Recker's mind was swirling as much as ever.

"We've been working a lot lately," Recker said. "Every day for the last few weeks. Feels like it's been around the clock."

"It's happened before."

"Maybe I just wanted to see something."

"Don't do this," Mia replied. "You saw it. Your eyes are perfect. Your mind is not gone. You didn't imagine it. He was there."

"But what if he wasn't?"

Mia put one of her hands on each side of Recker's face as she looked into his eyes. "Mike, you did not dream this up. Understand? I believe you. If you saw this guy, he was there. Keep working on it. You'll find him."

Recker gave her a smile, then kissed her on the lips. "Thanks."

"I will always believe in you. Always."

The following morning, Recker got up bright and early. He was ready to get into the office earlier than usual to continue his search on Marko Petrović. By the time he got there, he found his friends already knee-deep into it.

"What's the good word?" Recker asked.

Both Jones and Haley responded with a grimace and a shake of their heads. They hadn't come up with anything. Recker lowered his head.

"Nothing, huh?"

Not knowing what else to say, Haley just threw his hands up.

Jones detailed their searching. "I have tried to do a more thorough search, even putting Petrović's picture through the social media database to see if it matched up with any pictures found on there."

"Let me guess. You didn't."

"No, I didn't. His passport hasn't been used since that incident, no ID's, credit cards, transactions, nothing. I can't find a news article, dark websites mentioning his name, or anything along those lines. I can't find a single trace of his existence since that fateful day."

Recker took a deep breath as he looked toward the window. Things weren't off to a good start.

"What about the businesses at that building?"

"I've checked every single one," Haley answered. "On the outside, nothing looks out of the ordinary. You've got accounting firms, real estate brokerages, multiple medical offices, a marketing agency, design business, advertising agency, and several consulting firms. If there are any improprieties with any of them, I haven't found them yet."

Recker crossed his arm across his chest while he rubbed his face with his other hand. It was beginning to look like maybe the crazy part was winning out in this race. Jones and Haley turned back to their computers, continuing to put the work in. He could see it in their faces, though. They didn't want to say it yet.

But they had their doubts about all of this. How couldn't they? They were looking for a dead man. And there was no actual evidence that Petrović was still alive. Other than Recker thinking he saw them. And right now that was kind of shaky. Especially in Recker's mind.

"Anything else on the horizon?" Recker asked.

Jones quickly switched screens. "Nothing imminent."

"We don't have to keep checking on this. We can start up on other things again."

"We still have time to continue with this. Since there's nothing else going on, there's no harm in seeing if we can come up with something."

"Might not hurt to give Vincent a call," Haley said.

"What for?" Recker asked.

"If Petrović is in town, considering his history, there's a chance Vincent might know about him. Even if he's operating under an alias, he might know the face."

"That is a good point," Jones said.

Recker raised an eyebrow. "You're going to actually encourage me to meet with Vincent? That's a first."

Jones shrugged. "What can I say? The point is valid."

Recker knew they were right. If anyone had a handle on whether Petrović was actually in town, it would probably be Vincent. Nobody knew the criminal element in town like he did. But that would mean one more person he had to tell the story to. One more person that would look at him like he was crazy. Of course, maybe he didn't have to give all the details and backstory. He could probably talk in generalities.

Recker nodded at his partners without saying a word. He'd call Vincent. He'd see what the crime boss knew, if anything. But if he didn't, Recker wasn't sure where that would leave him. His mind was already going in a million different directions. If Vincent didn't know of Petrović, maybe Recker would have to answer some difficult questions. Maybe he really was seeing ghosts.

5

Recker was a little surprised when Vincent agreed to meet with him right away. Usually there was a little bit of a buffer. At least a couple of hours, if not a day or two. Especially on things that weren't urgent. This didn't qualify as that. Maybe to Recker it might, but it wouldn't to anyone else.

Recker was equally as surprised when the meeting place turned out to be somewhere other than the diner. That was usually where Vincent preferred to talk business. Instead, this time, they met down by the river.

By the time Recker got there, he saw Vincent sitting on a bench, watching a few ducks swim by. Malloy was just off to his right. And, of course, the rest of his men were scattered around standing guard not too far away. By now, Recker had a pass to go right through without the usual security protocols.

As he passed Malloy, he tapped him on the shoulder to greet him. Malloy motioned with his hand in response as Recker sat down next to Vincent. Recker briefly looked at the river, seeing the ducks, as well as a few boats go by. Malloy stepped further away so they could talk in private.

"Thanks for meeting me on short notice."

"Sure," Vincent said. "I happened to be in the area on other business, anyway. Just hopped on over. So what's on your mind?"

"Was wondering if you knew whether a certain man is in town."

"Got a name?"

"Marko Petrović. Croatian national."

Vincent looked down at the ground. "Petrović. Doesn't ring a bell off the top of my head. What are you looking for him for?"

"Let's just say... unfinished business."

Vincent smirked. "Sure."

"You're not doing business with him?"

"Not to my knowledge."

Recker took out an older picture of Petrović that they found from a newspaper article talking about his death. He handed it to Vincent.

"This is the guy."

Vincent appeared to carefully study the man's face. "Is this a recent photo?"

"No, it's about six or seven years old."

"Tough to say. A lot can change in six or seven years."

"His hair might be shorter," Recker said. "His face would be pretty similar."

Vincent continued giving the photo a good look. Nothing was coming to him, though. He handed the picture back.

"Can't say that he looks familiar."

"Thanks. Thought it might be worth a shot."

"So what's going on with him?"

"Well, if you do happen to come across him, you need to be on your guard. He might be going under a different name now, I don't know."

"I feel like the kid in the back of the class, watching all the other kids pass secrets to each other, but they never get around to the kid in the back. He gets left in the dark. It's kind of how I feel right now."

Recker took a second to figure out how he was going to answer, without making it seem like he was going crazy.

"Petrović is a guy I tangled with a long time ago. Before I ever moved here. He's very dangerous. Lethal. If he's actually in town, you need to be on your guard."

"And you think he's what... moving in to take me on?"

"I have no idea what his plans might be."

"You said, 'if he's actually in town'. You're not certain?"

"To be honest, no. Yesterday, I thought I saw him. I

thought I saw him. Now, maybe it was the sun, maybe things were moving, maybe I didn't get the best look. I don't know. But I thought I saw him. Now, in saying that, I haven't been able to find a shred of evidence that he's here. And we've looked. So, maybe he's not. Maybe I saw a mirage. But I just thought I'd check in with you first."

"I'm glad you did. Tell me about this guy."

"He's a mercenary, mostly. He'll work for anyone who pays him. But once he locks onto something, he does not let go. He is ruthless, and violent, and he will not let anyone or anything get in his way. He doesn't care if you're ninety years old, or nine. If you are in his way, you are a problem, and he will eliminate you without a second thought. He doesn't care."

"Sounds as though you've got quite the history with him."

Recker nodded. "Like I said, we've tangled a few times before. But, maybe I didn't really see him. I can't say with a hundred percent certainty. Not anymore."

"Anymore? You were, at one point?"

"I was convinced. When I locked eyes with him... it was him. There was no doubt. But now... now we can't find any trace of him. Nothing that indicates he's here."

"So now you're questioning yourself."

"Yeah, I guess so."

Vincent stared straight ahead, watching the ducks swim around in circles. "Look at those things. They move so gracefully above water, but underneath the surface, they're moving their legs like crazy under there. You can't see it, but those legs are moving a hundred miles an hour. They're working."

Recker didn't reply, not sure what Vincent was going on about. He was sure Vincent had a point that he'd eventually get to. Whatever it was.

"Always trust your instincts. Always. They've gotten you this far. Both of us. In our line of work, trusting, or not trusting, as the case may be, can either get you into hot water, or pull you out of it. I'd put your instincts above anybody's. Maybe even my own."

Recker grinned. "Thanks for that."

Vincent put his finger in the air. "You go at this like this man is here. Don't let anyone tell you otherwise. If you think you saw this man, then he is here until it's proven that he's not. That's the attitude that you have to have. No doubts. Doubts get people killed, as you well know."

Recker nodded. He didn't think he'd have Vincent giving pep talks for a hundred dollars on the bingo card today, but there they were. It was almost like a father giving his son a pep talk going into an important event. Recker appreciated the support.

"Have you heard of any upcoming threats?" Recker asked. "Maybe it's nothing that's big now, but maybe something that's simmering on the outside burner?"

Vincent chuckled. "Listen, this should come as no surprise to you, but when you're in my seat, it's always hot. There is always something that bears watching. Nothing that has come to an actionable level, though. But if this man is in town, and he's as bad as you say, I'll make sure to put some extra eyes and ears on the street."

"Just to be clear, if Petrović is here, I'm not saying he's gunning for you. He could be just passing through. Or maybe he's here on an unrelated issue. I just thought you should know, and maybe you'd heard something."

"I understand. Thank you for bringing it to my attention. Send a picture of the guy to Jimmy. I'll plaster his face to all of my boys to keep a lookout."

"Will do."

After Vincent and his men left, Recker remained on the bench, watching the activity on the river. He had nowhere else he had to be at the moment. Going back to the office to continue their search didn't exactly seem like it was producing any results. He sat there for half an hour, thinking about the situation he was now in, questioning whether he was right about anything. This was probably the most he ever doubted himself. Of course, seeing dead men would probably make anyone question themselves.

Just as he was about to get up, Recker's phone rang. After taking his phone out and seeing it was Lawson, he eagerly answered.

"Hey, didn't catch you at a bad time or anything, did I?"

"Nope," Recker answered. "Just watching some ducks."

"Ducks?"

"At the river."

"Oh. OK. I guess we all have our little things. Anyway, the reason I'm calling is I was able to get my hands on the Petrović file."

"And? Anything interesting?"

"Uh, yeah, you could say that. According to the file, Petrović is dead. And the file's considered closed."

"How's that interesting?"

"What's interesting is that I did some digging on some of the names I found in the file."

"OK?"

"This next stuff isn't in that file, because it's considered closed. So I went looking outside of that. You know the police officer that was sent to identify Petrović?"

"Yeah?"

"He was found dead three weeks later."

"Found dead?"

"Ruled a suicide."

"Nice coincidence," Recker said.

"The person that worked at the morgue died in a car accident one week after that."

"Coincidences are racking up."

"And there was a doctor that ruled Petrović dead to begin with."

"Well if we follow the pattern, I'd say there's a good chance that doctor's no longer with us."

"Correct," Lawson replied. "Only he was the first one to go. He died a week before the police officer did."

"How'd he go?"

"Apparently he was stabbed late at night in a rough part of town. Ruled a mugging."

"Taking care of loose ends."

"And they did a good job of it."

"Anyone else connected to it?" Recker asked.

"Those were the main guys listed."

"And now they're all dead. All within three weeks of Petrović supposedly being killed."

"Certainly does raise some questions."

"But does it prove that Petrović is still alive?"

"Not in itself," Lawson replied. "But it sure does make it seem sketchy."

"Anything on Petrović after that?"

"Not that I could find."

"What about a grave?"

"Cremated."

"Of course he was," Recker said. "Don't want it to be dug up later. Everything's nice and neat."

"That's the way to do it."

"So what's the unofficial word on these guys? Did we kill them?"

"Not that I can tell."

"And they all died under mysterious circumstances directly after the incident. Kind of makes you wonder."

43

"It does," Lawson said.

"But does that mean that Petrović is still alive and that he killed these other people to make sure that word never got out?"

"While I haven't seen anything to prove that's the case, I would also be a fool not to say that's how it looks."

"Still not proof," Recker said.

"Well, you saw him. I'd say that's proof."

"I thought I saw him."

"Well, combining that with what I've found, I'd say it's looking more like you were right."

"Still speculation. For all we know, Petrović was killed a month after that. We need something that proves he's been walking around all these years. Or for me to run into him again. And I'm not sure how likely that is."

"You want me to keep digging?" Lawson asked.

"If you can. I have a feeling you're not gonna find much, though."

"Maybe not. But if I can find an alias for Petrović, something that never got much traction, maybe we can start adding things up here."

"I appreciate it."

"What are you gonna do on your end?"

"Not sure. Coming up pretty empty on our end. Nothing's panning out."

"Maybe you need to narrow your search, then."

"How's that?"

"Where have you been looking?"

"Everywhere."

"Maybe that's the problem," Lawson said. "Narrow your focus. Where'd you see him going?"

"Into some office building."

"Scrap everything else. Don't check into anything other than that building. One of those businesses is not what they seem. Or they are, and Petrović had a very legit reason for being there. But one way or another, he was there for a reason. You just have to find it. Find that, then you find him."

After getting off the phone with Lawson, Recker continued sitting on the bench. He watched a couple of boats go by. Lawson was right. They did need to narrow their focus. So far, they were using the scattergun approach. They were all looking into different things, then moving on to something else if nothing caught their attention.

Even though Recker and Haley looked into the office building, they obviously didn't dig deep enough. There was something there. There had to be. Petrović didn't just blindly choose it on a whim. There was a reason. They just had to find out what that reason was.

6

Recker walked into the office, seeing Jones and Haley at the desk, both doing a lot of typing. A brief bit of hope swept through him, hoping they had found something.

"Somebody got something?"

"I'm afraid not," Jones replied, dashing his hopes.

"Oh."

"We might have another case coming up here. I'm watching it."

"Imminent?"

"Possible. Just waiting for one final thing. Could be soon."

"About our other thing... well, my other thing... and I was thinking that we should cut all searches off."

"Why?"

"It's not working and we're not finding anything,"

Recker said. "Plus, I feel like we're spreading things out instead of focusing on one thing."

Recker then let them know about the conversation he had with Lawson.

"That smells like a coverup if I ever heard one," Haley said.

"Smells fishy, don't it?"

"Extremely. Man gets killed, then the only people who can say it wasn't him wind up dead in the next few weeks? That sounds like a guy who wanted the world to think he was gone."

Jones folded his arms as he digested the news. "So Petrović, people close to him, pay off these other people to say he's dead? Then afterwards, he worries that they might have loose lips and give away the secrets, eliminate them so they can never talk?"

Recker nodded. "And nobody can ever say otherwise."

"That still leaves a lot of questions."

"You're telling me."

"So I can start digging into that day, see what I can put together, take it from there."

Recker quickly put the brakes on that. "Actually, I'm not sure that's a good idea."

Jones looked at him, confused. "If all this is true, that supports the idea that he's still alive. He'd have to leave a trace from that moment on."

"Actually, he wouldn't. And even if he did, that was

47

a long time ago. That's going to take a lot of time to go back seven years and figure it out from there."

"So are you just brushing this aside, then?"

"No. Let's focus on the here and now. I saw him going into that building. He was there for a purpose. We need to find out what that was."

"I checked into it," Haley said. "I couldn't find it."

"On the surface, probably nobody would. We need to dig deep. David, I figured you might be better to do that than anybody. That's what you're best at."

"I can start doing a deep dive on it," Jones replied.

Recker glanced over at Haley, whose eyes were looking away from him. He seemed to be staring at the wall.

"Chris? You good?" Recker asked.

Haley took a breath before answering. "There's a lot that don't add up here."

"Such as?"

"A man gets shot in the manner that he does, then a day later he's gone, with everyone who's verified that he's dead getting killed in the following couple of weeks? Add to that, he's never seen or heard from again until a chance encounter seven years later. That's some high-level stuff right there."

"I know."

Haley continued staring at nothing, causing Recker to think he still had more on his mind.

"Something else eating at you?"

"Quite a bit, actually," Haley answered.

"Wanna share?"

"Did you stick around that street after you shot him?"

"No, he went down, and I left," Recker said. "You know how it usually goes. A lot of chaos and confusion. The best time to slip away."

Haley nodded. "I know."

"What's bothering you?"

"This whole thing seems like it takes a lot of planning. A lot more than can be done in a chaotic time between the time being shot and people pronouncing him dead. A lot of moving parts. There's the ambulance that took him away, the people that identified him, plus getting a new identity on short notice, not to mention the fact that since he was shot, he'd need medical attention somewhere. And that was never reported either."

"So what are you getting at?" Recker asked.

"I'm not sure what happened could be done at a moment's notice."

"You think he'd been planning for that day all along?"

Haley shrugged. "It's possible. He could have had a contingency if he was ever shot, that these other things would come into play. Or there's another possibility."

"Which is?"

"That this was orchestrated by someone else."

"Orchestrated? How?"

"Someone needed Petrović dead, and you were sent to make that happen."

"But if he's not dead, then…"

"Everything's gone the way it was supposed to."

Recker stared at his friend, trying to read what he was thinking. After a little time, he thought he had it.

"Are you saying this was an agency-sponsored plan?"

Haley let out a small laugh. "It certainly wouldn't be the first time they did it. Think about it. If he knew you were out there, and since you tangled with him several times, he did, it's possible he could have been wearing a vest. And everyone else had their orders ahead of time."

"I didn't notice a vest on him."

"How long was he in your sights?"

"Not long."

Recker looked away for a moment, trying to get everything clear in his mind. "Why send me to do a job that you don't really want done?"

"Hey, maybe they didn't. Maybe Petrović had this in his back pocket the whole time."

"I have a theory, if I may?" Jones said, putting his hand up.

"We're not in class, David," Recker replied. "Just come out with it."

"Since you and Petrović battled on a few other

occasions before this final incident, is it possible he anticipated this, and figured he wasn't going to escape you by any other means, so the best way was to pretend that he was dead?"

"So he assumed I was going to shoot him at some point, and in the preceding days, lined up these other people to make sure he was found deceased?"

"Correct. Maybe there was no agency coverup. It could be you just got him worried from your previous encounters. So he took the necessary precautions."

Recker stroked his chin. He thought that notion was more likely. Not that he would have ruled out the CIA orchestrating this. After all, they double-crossed him not too long after that. He just wasn't sure what the reasoning would be for helping a notoriously dangerous thug like Petrović escape. But he also couldn't and wouldn't put it past them.

"How long were you on Petrović's tail?" Haley asked. "And how far apart were your other encounters with that last one?"

"I was on him a couple weeks. Three or four. And after one of our fights, he went out of sight for a few days. Got a tip he might be resurfacing to meet a contact at that market that was going on. So probably four or five days between sightings."

"Time enough to figure out an emergency plan. An exit strategy."

"Could be."

"I mean, even if he was able to thwart you, and disappear, he now knew the CIA was on his tail, right? So even if he got away, he knew they'd come back again. Somewhere down the line. So the best way to avoid that is to be dead. He made it known where he'd be, put a vest on, paid everyone else in advance, got a new identity in place, somewhere to hide out for a few days, then... disappeared."

"That's still leaving a lot to chance," Recker said.

"How so?"

"How'd he know I wouldn't shoot him in the head?"

Haley smirked. "Sometimes you gotta take chances. If he assumed he was dead regardless, might as well take the chance."

"Yeah, maybe."

"Assuming all that is correct, and it seems feasible that it is," Jones said. "How does that lead us to here? Seven years is a long time for someone of his stature to stay hidden."

"Maybe he took some time off. A year or so. Figured out his next steps. Then reemerged as someone else. And has just done enough to stay off the radar since then."

"I probably know the answer to this already, but is there any chance the reason he's been off the radar is because he's been clean all this time?"

Recker didn't even think about it. "No. No chance.

Trust me. This guy isn't capable of changing his stripes. He is what he is. And that's bad news."

"Well, I guess Ms. Lawson is correct, then. The key might be to finding out what he was doing inside that building. And I doubt he was just going for a stroll."

"One of those exemplary businesses is not what they appear to be."

"Could be for an innocent reason," Haley said. "Maybe he was just getting his taxes done. Or meeting with his social media manager. Or going through real estate listings with his agent."

Recker snickered. "Not likely."

"Well, assuming none of those scenarios is the real reason he's here, it would appear we have some digging to do," Jones said.

"Times like this I wish Tyrell was still in the business."

"We never did replace his ears on the street," Haley replied.

"Tough to find someone like him. Hard to trust someone as much as him. Plus, he knew everyone and everything, and people trusted him. It's just not the same without him."

"I bet he would've known what was going on. At least heard some rumblings and pointed us in the right direction."

"We have already got the right direction," Jones said. "That building is our compass. Now we just need it to show us the way."

The alert went off on Jones' computer. He quickly checked it, confirming it was the situation he had been monitoring.

"Looks like we've got trouble. Robbery going down in one hour."

Recker went over to the cabinet and took out a weapon. He also took out one for his partner and handed it to him. "What are we looking at?"

"Four men. All of them probably armed."

"Where?"

"Seedy motel."

Recker looked confused. "Seedy motel? We're not interrupting some drug buy, are we?"

Jones shook his head. "Business man. Clean record. Not married. No kids. Being lured there under the promise of sex."

"So basically a decent guy wanting to hook up for the night?"

"Basically. He's about to get a rude awakening. They're planning to rob him. They told him to bring five hundred dollars for the night."

"What about the four men?" Haley asked.

"All have records. All are violent. Don't roll up on this thinking it's a walk in the park."

"Never do."

Jones gave them the address of the motel, and Recker and Haley walked toward the door. They were already familiar with it, as they'd been there several times before. The only people that usually stayed there were criminals, drug dealers, and prostitutes. Visibility and lighting were very low in the complex. They also knew there were no cameras.

"Yeah, we're not the ones who've got trouble," Recker said. "They do."

7

Upon arriving at the motel, Recker and Haley had already figured out their plan. They weren't going to sit around and watch, waiting for the suspects to show up. Well, not on the outside, anyway. They obviously had to wait regardless, but they weren't going to do it sitting in the car. By the time they got up to the room, it might have been too late.

This time, they were going to do things a little differently. In this instance, they were already going to be in the room waiting for the men to arrive. Plus, it was the middle of the day, so they didn't want to be out in the open for too long.

They walked up the side steps that led to the second floor. They were looking for room 207. There was a railing to the left of them, overlooking the parking lot, as they walked along the concrete floor.

Once they found the room, Recker knocked. It didn't take long before it opened.

"I was so..." the grin quickly evaporated on the man's face once he saw the two men standing there instead of the blonde-haired, busty woman he thought he would see.

"Yeah, me too," Recker replied.

"Uh, you're not... uh, what do you want?"

"We're here for you, stupid."

Recker pushed the door open, and he and Haley walked in. The man looked kind of stunned, not sure what was going on.

"You can't just... you can't come in here."

Once Recker was in the middle of the room, he turned around. "Close the door."

The man did a double take, then did as he was directed. Recker was in the middle of the room, while Haley was just off to the man's left, by the window. He peeked out to make sure their visitors hadn't gotten there yet. They still had about ten minutes if they came on time.

The shocked man put his arms out. "Who are you? What is going on here? What are you doing? What do you want?"

"A lot of questions there, and not a lot of time," Recker answered. "Basically, you're about to be robbed."

The man's face turned from shock to worry in an instant. "Look, wait, I don't really..."

Recker put his left hand out. "Not by us. We're here to prevent it."

The man suddenly breathed a sigh of relief. "What are you, the police or something?"

"We'll go with the or something."

"How do you know I'm about to be robbed?"

"Look, you're not here meeting who you think you are."

The man hesitated, not wanting to admit he was only there for sex. "Uh... what... what do you mean?"

"We really don't care that you thought you were here for a booty call. You thought you were communicating with a woman. You weren't. You were really talking to a crew of four guys. Well, one guy, I suppose. He's with a group of four, all of whom are dangerous. They do this type of thing. They get unsuspecting men and women to come to a spot where they think they're meeting someone."

"Only there's no booty waiting for them," Haley said.

"That's right. Instead, these four thugs are waiting. And they're gonna take everything you got. Well, whatever you got with you. Cash, credit cards, everything. Then they'll probably tie you up for a bit while they're out running up your credit card for things they can fence later. By the time you get out and can dispute the charges, you're already down a few thousand dollars."

The man looked stunned, hardly believing this was

happening. All he wanted was a little companionship for a few hours. Now here he was in the middle of whatever this was.

"How do you know all this? Were you guys spying on me? Is that legal?"

Recker rolled his eyes. Here they were telling him he was about to be robbed, and he was only wondering if they were here under legal circumstances.

"Look, Sparky, we know this because we've been monitoring the communication between these guys. They made plans to rob someone, they all talked amongst each other, and that someone turned out to be you. So here we are."

The man walked over to a chair and sat down, his shoulders slumped, looking down at the floor. He looked despondent.

"I can't believe this."

"Most people can't," Recker replied.

"If it makes you feel better, it's not really you," Haley said. "It's nothing you did. You just were unfortunate enough to stumble into it."

"Doesn't really make me feel better."

Haley shrugged. "Worth a shot."

"So what do we do here?"

"We wait for them to show up," Recker answered.

"That's it? That's your plan?"

"Yep."

"Do you have other guys outside?"

"Nope."

"Didn't you say there's four of them?"

"Yep."

Worry started creeping over the man's face. Even more than was already there to begin with. "Soo... there's nobody else except you two?"

"That's it."

"And there's four of them? But only two of you?"

Recker sighed, tiring of the questions. "Yeah, listen, this is kind of our specialty. We're not worried."

"So what are you going to do?"

"Fix the problem. That's what we do."

"How?"

"Let us worry about that."

"Do they already know what you look like?" Haley asked.

"Uh, yeah. I sent over a picture of me."

"That takes out one of us posing as you and answering the door."

"So what's that mean?"

"It means when there's a knock on the door, you've gotta answer," Recker replied.

"What? Seriously? I thought you said these guys were dangerous."

"They are."

"So why do I have to answer the door?"

"Because if one of us do it, they'll know it's a trap. Then they might scatter before we have a chance to do anything. Then they can do it again to the next person that comes along. And the cycle continues. We obviously need to stop that."

"How? How are you going to do that when you're outnumbered?"

Recker grinned. "We have our ways."

"I don't really want to do this."

"You don't really have a choice."

"What if they come in?"

"That's what we want."

"What?!" The man was starting to breathe funny and began to hyperventilate. "I don't know if I can do this."

Recker knew they had to calm him down before he became completely useless. They didn't really need him for much. But he couldn't be a blubbering idiot before they put their plan into action.

"Look, calm down and relax before you pass out. All we need you to do is open the door. That's it. Once they come in, we'll do the rest."

"What if they do something to me first?"

"They won't. They'll most likely first ask you where your money and wallet is. They'll try it the easy way first."

"But what if they don't?"

"Then we'll be right here. Trust me, you'll be fine if you do what we tell you."

"Why don't you have more people here?"

Recker snapped his fingers. "Focus. When the door knocks, go over and open it. That's all you have to do."

"And where will you guys be?"

Recker took a look around. "Well, there's a closet right there and a bathroom over there. So that's where we'll be."

"What if there's shooting?"

"Duck, drop to the floor, and crawl under the bed until it's over."

"Oh my God. What did I get myself into? All I wanted was a couple hours of sex. That's it. And now I'm somehow dodging bullets and meeting bad guys."

Haley continued peeking out the window, looking in both directions, waiting for a sign that things were about to go down. He glanced at the time.

"Should be any minute now."

No sooner had he said it, he then noticed a couple of people at the top of the steps to his left.

"This might be it."

Recker instantly moved over to the closet, ready to duck inside.

"Wait, this might not be them. There's a woman with them."

"How many?" Recker asked.

"Five."

"Maybe there really is a woman with them. Just for show."

"Possible, I guess. See which way they're heading. They're coming this way."

They stopped just in front of the unit, and there was a knock on the door. Haley immediately ran over to the bathroom.

"Guess that answers that question," he whispered.

As he ducked into the bathroom, Recker jumped into the closet. Neither of them closed the doors fully. They wanted to be able to spring out at a moment's notice and surprise the group. Recker peeked out through the sliver of the door that was open, and noticed their friend taking a deep breath. It looked like the man didn't really want to go through with it. He didn't really have any choice now, though. They were there. And they weren't going away.

After it looked like he sucked up enough courage, the man went over to the door and opened it. He was surprised to see a good-looking blonde standing there.

"Well it took you long enough," she said with a smile.

"Nice to see you."

Another guy suddenly came into the frame and delivered a knockout blow, sending the unsuspecting man to the floor. Then, the four people went inside, stepping over the man's body, and closing the door. Two of the gang picked the man up by the arms and dragged him along the floor, propping him up against the end of the bed.

"First off, I'm so sorry," the woman said. "I really hate this part of it. But it kind of is... just how it goes, you know?"

Recker patiently waited, wanting all of the gang to have their backs to him if possible. That would give him a clear advantage. But he was willing to forego that if he had to. He'd give it another minute or two.

A bald man, who appeared to be in his fifties, seemed to be in control of the group. He spoke up first.

"As you can see, you're not getting lucky today. But there's two ways this can go here, OK? You can give us your wallet, money, credit cards, valuables, all that... and then we'll tie you up and get out of here. But at least you'll be alive and unhurt, right? We won't even rough you up."

The woman clapped her hands excitedly. "Get to the other part."

The man smiled. "Or, you can play the tough guy, and pretend you don't got nothing, and then we'll beat you to a bloody pulp. Then after we've had our fun with you, we'll rip this room apart until we got what we came for, anyway. So it really all depends on you. I'm actually OK doing it either way."

The man on the floor held his face. "Whatever you want."

The bald man smiled again. This was old hat to him. "Good. Now, where's your wallet and valuables?"

That was Recker's cue. None of the group was paying attention to anything other than the man on the floor, thinking they had a pretty easy score here. And while they all didn't have their backs to Recker, it was close enough. Two of them did, while the other two had their side facing the closet. It would do.

Recker burst out of the closet, holding his gun out in front, ready to drop anyone who might have been dumb enough to try something. They all turned and looked at him, completely shocked at what was transpiring. As soon as Haley heard his partner moving, he did the same, scurrying out of the bathroom.

The three men, and one woman, looked completely clueless as they saw the two men pointing guns at them. This was not how it was supposed to go down.

"What's going on?" the woman asked.

"We're the neighborhood watch," Recker replied.

The bald man snickered. "That's pretty good. Neighborhood watch. I like that."

Recker smiled. "Good. Maybe you guys can form your own group where you're going."

"Oh? And where's that?"

"Prison."

"What would we go there for?"

Recker pointed to the man on the floor, still holding his face. "Uh, should we add up the charges so far? Let's see... assault, attempted robbery, you all have records, so having a gun on you is another no-no."

The man put his hands out. "What robbery? We didn't rob nobody."

"I'm pretty sure you broke in here with the intent of

relieving him of his valuables. I heard you say as much."

The man laughed. "I was just joking. We're old friends. And what are you doing hiding inside a closet? I think that's entrapment."

"Yeah, except it's not. And we're not cops anyway."

"Oh, you're not? Then what are you?"

"Just concerned citizens trying to make a difference."

"Oh, you're a bunch of goody-goodies. Doesn't change anything. We're not going to jail. And you're gonna let us walk out of here."

"Why would I let you do that?" Recker asked.

"Because if you don't, we're gonna kill you."

Recker briefly looked at his partner, wondering if they had some secret weapon they didn't know about. It certainly didn't look like the gang had anything working in their favor.

"There's four of you. We've got guns on you. Don't try to pull them. You'll never make it."

"Well, see, here's the thing. We're not going to jail. So if you intend to put us there, we're gonna have a problem."

"If we let you leave here, I don't suppose I could get your word that you'd change your ways and become upstanding citizens, huh?"

The bald man smirked. "Oh, yeah, that's exactly what we'll do. In fact, as soon as we leave here, I'm gonna head to church. And then I'll say a few Hail Mary's, and maybe an Our Father or two. And then I'm gonna really look at my life and see the error of my ways. Then maybe I'll become a social worker and help the needy. I'm gonna do all of it. You have my word."

The look on Recker's face indicated he was amused. The man was obviously being sarcastic, not that he really expected any different.

"Where's the other guy?" Haley asked.

"What other guy?"

"There's supposed to be four of you."

"Are there? Gee, nobody told me I was supposed to bring another guy. Sorry, fellas. So can we go now? I wanna get to the church before it closes."

"Not yet," Recker said. "First, I want all of you to drop your guns."

"We're not packing."

Recker chuckled. "You're really something, aren't you?"

"I just wanna be honest."

"You want to do this the hard way, huh?"

"No, I sure don't, sir. I'm just telling you the truth. This was just supposed to be an easy job, so we didn't figure there was a need for that extra stuff. And that's the truth."

"Sure it is."

"So can we go now?"

"No, you're going to jail," Recker answered.

"See, that's a problem. Cause we're not going. And you're not gonna make us."

"I beg to differ."

The group didn't seem to be all that concerned that there were guns pointed at them. They still seemed very confident. That was a little bit of a red flag for Recker. It was almost like the gang didn't consider them a threat at all. Or they had something else up their sleeve. Recker wasn't sure what that could have been, except for one thing. The fourth man that was missing. He had to be lurking nearby. They had to be waiting for him.

Then, almost on cue, the front door swung open. The fourth man they were looking for appeared. Recker instinctively dropped to a knee and turned toward the man. Recker saw a gun in his hands. The man fired, the bullet flying over Recker's head, though it would have hit him right in the chest if he hadn't dropped to a knee first.

Recker returned fire, drilling the man in the stomach. As that was going on, the rest of the men started reaching for their weapons. The bald man took his gun out and aimed for Recker, but Haley shot him two times in the chest. He quickly took aim at the next guy, who seemed like he was frazzled and not sure what to do or who to aim at. Haley took care of him without a problem. Then Recker swung back around and nailed the remaining man, putting him on the ground with one shot.

With all of their adversaries taken care of, Recker stood up again. The woman was still standing there, her eyes closed, holding both sides of her head, and screaming her head off. Recker and Haley glanced at each other, then looked at her. She just kept screaming, either not sure that the fight was over, or just scared out of her mind and having a reaction. In either case, Recker didn't want to listen to it anymore. He tapped her on the arm.

"It's over."

The woman opened her eyes and stopped screaming. She looked down and saw all the dead bodies of her friends. She immediately put her hands on her head and started screaming again. Recker and Haley looked at each other, both of them shaking their heads. Recker put his hands on the woman's arms, bringing them down.

"Hey!"

The woman was wide-eyed, thinking she was about to meet the same fate as her friends.

"I don't even have a gun!"

"We know that," Recker said. "That's why you're still standing."

"Oh. What are you gonna do with me?"

"I dunno. What do you think we should do with you?"

"Um. Let me go?"

"Why should we do that?"

"Because I promise to never ever do something like this again. Like, I really promise. Like, forever."

Recker tilted his head, giving her a face like he didn't believe her. "But won't you?"

The woman shook her head. "No. I promise. I swear. I mean it."

Recker had his doubts, but he really didn't care about her all that much. He didn't know anything about her. She wasn't even supposed to be there. For all he knew, she had a clean record. Of course, maybe she didn't. But he wasn't going to waste any more time there and find out. Gunshots, even at a seedy place like the spot they were in, had a habit of drawing the police in a hurry.

"Get out of here," Recker told her.

The woman instantly ran out the front door.

"Guess we should be doing the same," Haley said.

Recker nodded. They put their guns away and started toward the door. The man on the floor finally got up, looking at all the dead bodies around him.

"Hey, what about me?"

The Silencers turned around.

"What about you?" Recker asked.

"What am I supposed to do?"

"Wait for the police to show up."

The man put his arms out. "With all this?"

"Just tell them what happened."

"What about you guys?"

"We're leaving."

"Why?"

"The police sometimes aren't fond of us," Recker answered.

The man pointed to his eye. "But what about my face?"

"Looks like just a bruise. Ask for some medical attention and you'll be fine."

"That's it? You're gonna go, just like that?"

"Yep. That's how we always do it. Just like that."

8

Recker and Haley got back to the office, and Jones was already waiting for them. They had told him how the mission went, so there was no need to rehash it. But Jones had some other things on his mind. He started peppering Recker with questions before he even got the door closed.

"What are the chances that Petrović has a twin brother?"

Recker pulled his head back, the way people usually do when they've heard an outlandish idea. "A twin brother? Seriously?"

"What? I'm just asking. Is it really out of the question?"

"Are we living in some kind of soap opera or something? We got rid of the character and now we're gonna bring back an evil twin that nobody's ever heard of?"

"Hard to be more evil than Petrović," Haley said.

"That's true."

"I'm just making sure we have all our bases covered," Jones said. "I know twins are rare, but they're out there. I just want to make sure."

"No, I get it," Recker said. "But no, he doesn't have a twin. The information packet I got on him when I did the job indicated he was an only child."

"Any chance that information packet could have been incorrect?"

"Is there a chance?" Recker shrugged. "Sure, I guess there's a chance. Right now I'm questioning everything involved in that assignment. But to my knowledge, there's no twin. And no brother at all."

Jones swiveled his chair around to face his computer again. "Just thought I'd ask."

"I guess I shouldn't ask how everything's going on your end of things. If you're asking about twin brothers, I kind of get the feeling you're grasping at straws."

"Just making sure no stone is left unturned."

Recker sighed. "Yeah."

As Recker walked over to get a drink, Haley sat down at a computer and started typing. He seemed to have a specific purpose in mind. Jones glanced over at him.

"Something on your mind?"

"Yeah," Haley replied. "Something."

"Would you like to share?"

"Checking all airports, bus stations, trains, etcetera. If Petrović is here, it's likely he hasn't been here all that long. Guys like him don't usually stay in one spot. I'd say probably within the last two weeks."

"We already checked all that," Jones said. "We didn't come up with anything."

"I know. Maybe we were looking in the wrong place."

Jones looked at him curiously. And Recker, over-hearing the conversation, walked over to the desk, a bottle of soda in hand. He was intrigued, hoping his partner had stumbled onto something.

"You think we missed something?" Recker asked.

Haley didn't reply at first. He started to make a head movement, but then started waffling. "Eh, not so much missed. Maybe looked in the wrong spot to begin with."

"I don't follow your meaning," Jones said.

"Well, we obviously know Petrović hasn't been here for long, right? I mean, a guy like him, we obviously would've run into him long before this if he'd been here for any length of time."

"Right."

"So that means he must have just gotten here recently."

"Yes, and we already checked the airport, trains, buses, and so forth."

"But I'm betting we checked the wrong ones."

Jones gave him a crazy look. "How many airports do you think there are in this city?"

"It's not this city I'm concerned about."

Jones looked up at Recker, wondering if he had any clue what was going on. Recker wasn't saying anything. And Jones couldn't tell by the look on his partner's face as to whether he understood what was happening or not.

Jones wasn't done asking questions. "What exactly is it that you're looking for, that we didn't already search for?"

Haley stopped typing for a moment to turn toward his friends. "Look, Petrović is an All-World bad guy, right? And if he's been in the shadows for this long, it means he knows how to blend in, right?"

"So far I follow you."

"That means taking extra precautions, and not doing anything that can be easily tracked, traced, or spotted."

"Still following."

"So thinking along those lines, if I was him, and I had any kind of business here, knowing my past history, am I just going to fly into PHL and do my thing?"

"No," Recker answered, sensing where his partner was going.

Haley nonchalantly pointed at him. "Right. I wouldn't even fly in here at all. Or bus, or train, or any of that."

"You'd use a different entry point."

"Right."

Jones tried to make sense of it. "So you're saying

that Petrović would have flown into another airport, and then drove here?"

"Well, not necessarily flown," Haley replied. "Could've gone another way, but basically that's what I'm saying."

"Makes sense," Recker said.

"OK, I can see that," Jones said. "But that's still a lot to unpack. I mean, if you figure that is the case, and it certainly is valid, that's still a lot of places to check."

"I figure... check all methods of transportation within a... three-hour drive from here?" Haley asked.

"I'd double it," Recker responded. "Petrović doesn't play by normal conventions. If we think three, he'll do more."

Haley nodded, agreeing. "Six, it is."

Jones still had more reservations, even though he agreed with the point in principle. "As sound as an idea as that is, and I don't question the logic at all, there is one other point that needs to be made that could throw some cold water on all of it."

"And what's that?"

"You're assuming that Petrović just got here within the last few weeks. And I don't just mean Philadelphia. I mean the whole country."

Recker sighed, knowing his partner had made a valid point. "What if he's been lying low for months?"

"Or years. There's no guarantee he's been in Europe all this time and just got here recently. For all we know, he might have been here all this time."

Recker hit the table in frustration. It wasn't a hard blow, and it wasn't forceful. But he turned around and walked over to the window to look out into the parking lot.

"Hey, we won't know unless we try," Haley said. "Let's just run it this way, see what pops up."

"What parameters will you use?" Jones asked.

"I'll put the facial rec software on every airport, bus station, train station, and every other station that has a camera within a six-hour radius from here."

"Do you need my assistance?"

Haley put his hand up, as if to shoo him away. "I've got it, I've got it. You've shown me how to work it enough times. I can do it."

Jones smiled. "Do you think it more likely Petrović would come through via a big airport or a small one? Assuming that's his method of entry."

"Could make a case for either," Recker said, turning around. "A big airport, or big anything, there's the appeal of blending in with a large amount of people. Harder to spot. But that still means a large number of people. Things can happen, you get spotted, a bad break, something along those lines. In theory, a small place is easier to hide, unless, of course, that place is under surveillance. Then you'll stick out more."

"Which would you choose?"

"I'd pick the easiest spot where I wouldn't have to

worry about being spotted. No cameras. Limited number of people, if any."

"So the search could very well be a big waste of time."

"Could be. But not everyone thinks like me."

Jones grinned. "I suppose that is something to be thankful for."

"Well, we'll see in a few hours what's what," Haley said. "Hopefully, Petrović made a mistake somewhere."

"Assuming he's actually alive and out there," Recker said, allowing his doubts to show.

"He's out there. All that nonsense at his supposed death, that's a coverup if I ever saw one."

Recker turned back to the window. "So it would seem. But it's not proof. And that's something we don't have."

"Yet," Jones replied. "Something we don't have yet. But we're working on it. Sooner or later, we'll come up with something. We always do."

They always had up to that point. But as Recker gazed out the window, his eyes looked up to the sky. It was a slightly overcast day. Appropriate for the times, he thought. What if this was one of the times they couldn't? Nine years was a lot of time to go through on such short notice. They usually didn't have to cover that much of a gap.

And for all they know, Petrović was already here and gone. Maybe he was just passing through, or only staying for a day or two. Perhaps he'd already gotten what he needed here and was already in some other city. That would mean they were doing a lot of searching for nothing. What they needed was a break. Some type of luck.

Recker stared up at the sky again, seeing more dark clouds roll in. He took a deep breath as he thought about the situation. That's what they needed. A lucky break. But it sure didn't seem like they were going to get it.

9

The facial recognition software continued to run for the next couple of hours. So far, they didn't get any hits. Not even a partial hit. Not even a five-percent match that they could run down. It wasn't looking promising. It seemed to be par for the course.

Recker was antsy and was hoping they had some other cases coming down the pike. He didn't want to just wait and stew over things.

"Anything on the horizon?" Recker asked.

Jones shifted his focus and pulled up a different screen. He shook his head. "No. Nothing else is imminent."

Recker sighed as he started to pace. Jones watched him for a moment, knowing what his pacing usually meant.

"We all know things can happen in a jiffy, though.

Nothing imminent now could turn into a full-blown fire in five minutes."

It didn't lighten Recker's mood. "Yeah. Great."

Jones knew to just let his partner be for a few minutes. He'd come around after stewing about it for a bit. Recker's phone rang, and he was a bit surprised when he saw the ID. He wasn't expecting Lawson to call him for anything.

"Is there something I can do for you?"

"It's not what you can do for me," she said. "It's what I can do for you."

"And what's that?"

"Give you some information."

"About Petrović?"

"How'd you guess?"

"It's a specialty of mine."

Lawson laughed. "I bet. Anyway, I've been doing some more digging."

"Come up with any dirt?"

"Oh, lots and lots of dirt."

"What do you have?"

"Well, just to give you some context, I went back through Petrović' history, and looked at everything he's ever done."

"That must've taken a while," Recker said.

"It did. Knowing a leopard doesn't change his spots, I started doing a statistical analysis, and employed a bunch of people here who are smarter than me, and we started doing some computer models."

"What?"

"Basically, we used Petrović's history, and then projected that, assuming he was still living, based on other incidents that we know about that have actually happened since his supposed death."

"OK. I think I'm following you."

"So based on past history, you can see what the likelihood of those incidents happening in the future."

"Yeah, I got it."

"So using that as a basis, we started studying those incidents to see if any could be traced back to him."

"Any luck so far?" Recker asked.

"It's pretty interesting. There's obviously thousands of incidents to look at over the last nine years. Now, some we could immediately discount. We know exactly who did them, and there was no doubt about it."

"And the others?"

"Well, there was no known player that we could identify in some of them. And in others, there was a name, but not much more than that."

"I get the feeling there's something you're trying to tell me with all this," Recker said.

"Basically, I think I got him."

"Petrović?"

"He's alive," Lawson replied. "At least I think so."

Recker's skin started tingling upon hearing the news. "How do you know?"

"I'll try to cut this to the short version."

"I'd appreciate that."

"Anyway, we started looking into a bunch of different names, and I'm talking hundreds, to see if there were any profiles that were similar. And then we started getting some matches. Now, some were just similarities, nothing more to it, and that's obviously going to happen. You know, you look into it, see that it's obviously someone else, that's it."

"Yeah?"

"And then you get to some and you just scratch your head. Because there's not much out there on them. Basically, to cut this short like I said, we found one name that had a very similar MO to Petrović, that did everything almost identically."

"What happened to the short version?"

Lawson chuckled. "I know. It's just exciting. Anyway, Petrović, there was one name we found, that when we did some digging, we couldn't find a history on."

"Meaning?"

"Meaning... when we looked into the name, the earliest reference we could find on it went back to one month after Petrović was killed. Supposedly."

"So you couldn't find any trace of this man before that?"

"Nope. We've tried everything. We can't find any piece of paper, any reference, nothing... until one month after that incident."

"Promising lead. Good chance it's a fake identity

just created in that time period."

"Exactly."

"Still doesn't prove that it's him, though. As much as I want to believe it, and even if it looks that way, it still isn't proof."

"I agree," Lawson said. "Not in and of itself. But there's more."

"What do you have?"

"A picture."

"You got him on camera?"

"It's not a great picture, but it's something. I'm sending it over to you now."

As soon as Recker heard the alert go off on his phone, he opened the message. He saw the picture of the man Lawson was referencing. Like she warned, it wasn't a great picture. But it wasn't a terrible one, either. The man was wearing a hoodie, and a baseball hat, and he was standing to the side of the camera, so it wasn't a full-on view. But it was something.

"What do you think? Look like Petrović to you?"

Recker took another glance at it. "Could be. Got the same build. Tough to see the face clearly. Hair is different. But that matches the person I saw the other day. When was this taken?"

"About three years ago. He's been on our watchlist, but there's very little on him, so we're still gathering information about him."

"What name's he going under?"

"Jakov Horvat."

Recker raised an eyebrow. "Still Croatian?"

"It's smart, when you think about it."

"Maybe. If anyone ever comes looking for him, they'd assume he'd change his name to something else completely. The last thing they'd think is that he went from a Croatian name to another Croatian name."

"Exactly. Just think about it from our perspective. Whenever someone in our line of work assumes a new identity, it's almost always from a different country. You want to put your past life as far in the rearview mirror as possible. He had to figure that if his stunt about still being alive was found out, nobody would still look there."

"Petrović was never a dumb guy."

"Do you have tabs on where this Horvat is now?"

"No. The last report we have on him is from six months ago."

"Where was he then?" Recker asked.

"Serbia."

Recker sighed. There still wasn't any proof. Names, pictures, suspicions, none of it added up to a guarantee, or anything that resembled proof positive.

"What's wrong?"

"Because everything is just... we're still speculating."

"I'm convinced. Why aren't you? You're the one that brought this to me."

"I know. And I'm thankful for the work you've done on it. I'm just... I don't know."

"You're doubting yourself. Aren't you?"

"Well, I mean, I guess a person would tend to do that when they see someone who they thought they killed almost a decade ago."

"Yeah, I guess they would. I really do think we're on the right track here, though."

"You don't have any idea of where Horvat might be now?"

"None."

"And you don't have any other pictures of him?"

"Just that one," Lawson said. "He's an elusive guy."

"Any other aliases associated with him?"

"Not that we've found so far. We'll keep digging, though."

"All right. I guess it's a start. It's not the slam dunk I was hoping for, but I guess it's a start."

"You should know... there's very few of those in this business. You take the breadcrumbs when you can get them and start piecing things together from there. Eventually, you put all those crumbs together and you might have something."

"It's just a question of whether that something is what I'm looking for," Recker replied.

"The charts are saying it is."

"I'm not a real big chart guy."

"I know, I know. Look, I'll keep digging. But I just wanted to give you the name, maybe you can run with it too. Between the both of us, maybe we'll get to where we wanna go sooner."

"That's the hope. Thanks. We'll start looking into it."

"No problem. If I get anything else, I'll let you know."

Recker hadn't even shoved his phone in his pocket before he started getting hit with questions. Jones was listening to his conversation and was intrigued by it.

"That sounded somewhat hopeful."

Recker looked at both of his partners, hesitating for a second. "Lawson believes Petrović is still alive."

Jones and Haley glanced at each other for a moment. By the looks on their faces, they were surprised to hear it.

"She knows that for a fact?" Jones asked.

"Suspects it more than knows it."

"What kind of information does she have?" Haley asked.

Recker waved a hand in the air. "Uh, it's a little complicated. There's a bunch of charts and analysis and comparisons and... you know... stuff. You know how the nerds like to do it." He then looked at Jones. "No offense."

"So she's basing it all on statistical analysis?"

"Basically. I mean, they're running such advanced stuff there, I won't even pretend to understand it all. You know how it is."

"Yeah. Well, she's not just waving her hand in the air. If based on their computer models, they say he's still alive, then he is."

"What are they basing it on?" Jones asked.

"There's this one name they found. Jakov Horvat. They can't find any existence of him before Petrović was supposed to be killed. The identity didn't come online until one month later."

"A nice coincidence," Haley said.

"All the charts say that Horvat mirrors the patterns and movements of Petrović. And they have one picture of him."

Recker took his phone out again and showed each of his partners the picture Lawson sent him.

"Not a great shot," Haley said.

"Is that all they had?" Jones asked.

"It's all they got," Recker answered.

"Could be him," Haley replied.

"Could be."

Jones immediately started typing. "Let me start running the name."

"Knowing Petrović, if this is the same guy, it's not likely you'll come up with much."

"Perhaps not, but it's worth checking."

Recker turned toward the window and looked out. "Yeah. But I still think the key resides in that office building somewhere."

"I'm still looking into it. If there's something there, I'll find it. Eventually."

"Yeah. Eventually. That's what I'm worried about. Finding it after it's too late."

10

The crew was working late into the night, not that they were having much success with anything. Jones was working on finding some irregularities with one of the businesses in that office building that Petrović entered. But he wasn't finding anything yet. Recker and Haley were looking manually checking flight manifests, bus fares, trains, everything up and down the east coast, hoping Petrović would stick out somewhere. No luck on that front, either. And Petrović's face hadn't popped up on their facial scan software. Either the man was truly a ghost, and he was as good at blending in as anyone they had come across, or they had everything wrong. Such as the man being alive to begin with.

Frustrated, Recker got up from the desk and started walking around the room. Everyone seemed to believe him now about Petrović being alive. Lawson believed it, Jones and Haley seemed to think there was a good chance, even Mia thought so. But Recker was still having his doubts. With every hour that passed without finding anything, the more doubt creeped into his mind. Everyone seemed to have more faith in what he saw now except for him.

He just couldn't shake the feeling that maybe it was somehow all in his mind. Maybe everyone was on the wrong trail. What if the computer readouts that Lawson was getting were all wrong? It was just an analysis of probabilities. Even if the computers were predicting a seventy or eighty percent match, that still left a possibility that they were incorrect. And without any kind of visual confirmation, other than Recker's own eyes, which he didn't trust, there was still a doubt.

For Recker to feel better about all of this, he really needed something more concrete than a CIA computer analysis. He realized they were usually pretty good, but they weren't perfect. Or infallible. He desperately wanted to lock eyes with Petrović again. Just for his own peace of mind.

Some people might have questioned why it even mattered to him at this point. After all the time that elapsed, some people might have suggested just to move on. He did the job that he was supposed to do at the time. That should have been the end of it.

But that's not how Recker's mind worked. For him,

if Petrović really was alive, then it wasn't the end of it. The mission was still ongoing. One of the things that made Recker as good as he was, was the ability to see everything he worked on come to a conclusion. He couldn't leave something up in the air. That irked him.

If Petrović was still breathing, that meant he never finished the job he was supposed to do. That would wear on him for the next several years if he didn't find a solution. He'd worry about all the innocent people that lost their lives at Petrović's hands in the last nine years. People that should be enjoying their life with their significant other, or playing with their kids, or making a difference in society. But now, they only had someone grieving over them because Recker didn't finish the job. That's the part that wore on him the most. The people that were no longer here. And if Petrović was still out there after all this time, he knew that number was significant.

"Anything else happening anywhere?" Recker asked.

"In regards to what?" Jones replied.

Recker pointed to the window. "Out there. The usual stuff. The people that we usually try to help."

Jones sensed his friend's frustration and tried to help put him at ease. "Still nothing on the horizon at the moment. Don't worry, we're not taking attention away from anything else. If something pops up or needs more investigating, we'll handle it."

"I just wanna make sure we're not... distracted."

"We are fine. Why don't you go home, spend some time with Mia, go see a movie, go to dinner, do something to take your mind off things?"

"Mia's working."

"Oh. Well then, go home, put on some music and zen out."

"Yeah, because I do that so well."

"Michael, you need to stop putting a hole in the carpet. Everything will sort itself out. There is no sense in worrying over what you cannot control."

"I just wanna get this over with. One way or the other."

"And it will. Nine years is a lot of time to make up. Especially with a case such as this. But we'll get there."

"If you tell me it's just going to take time, I'm gonna come over there and slap you."

Jones snickered. "Noted. Noted. But it will."

Recker gave him a glare. The evil look was interrupted by the sound of his phone ringing. He saw it was Malloy and answered.

"What's going on?"

"You might wanna come down here," Malloy replied.

"Where's here? And why?"

"Here is the warehouse on 75th. Why... we might have something that interests you."

"Are you gonna give me any hints?" Recker asked.

"It might have something to do with the guy you're looking for."

"What? You found him?"

"I can't say definitely. I can say it looks possible."

"What's going on?"

"Well, we got a tip from one of our informants that there's a shipment of... well... let's just say... illegal contraband. And it just came into the warehouse."

"What's that got to do with the guy I'm looking for?"

"Maybe everything, maybe nothing. Can't say for sure. But the tip we've got is that the person behind this shipment is a European. Eastern Europe, to be exact. Isn't that where your guy is from?"

"Croatia, yeah."

"Apparently, not much is known about this guy, according to our source. He's a big, mysterious type of guy. Our contact says the guy's got a mean streak."

"Your contact have a name to go with this European?" Recker asked.

"Nah. From what he understands, a lot of people are afraid of this guy. Says he's... different. Smart, cunning, ruthless."

"Sounds like my guy."

"In any case, people just refer to him by a nickname."

"What's that?"

"Solin."

Recker's eyes immediately lit up. He was familiar with the name. "That's not a nickname."

"That's what everyone's referring to the guy as."

"Solin is a city."

"Oh. Where's that?"

"Croatia."

"Sounds like you know it already."

"I had to do a lot of research on Petrović when I was looking for him before. Solin is the city where he was born."

"Oh. Wow. OK. Sounds like maybe that's not a coincidence, then."

"Yeah. Sounds like it's not. You have eyes on this guy right now?"

"Well, it's hard to know what we're looking for," Malloy answered. "Right now, we're looking at a warehouse, with a small crew standing on the outside of it. Just two guys. Might be another one inside. We've been here for a while and watched as the truck came in, dropped off their load, then left. We didn't wanna make a move yet until I let you know."

"OK, thanks."

"From what I can see, it doesn't look like whoever's in charge is here. Maybe I'm wrong, but it seems like they're waiting for someone. Whether that guy is your guy, or the guy in charge, who knows? Maybe it'll turn out to be nothing. And whether he shows up tonight is another story altogether."

"He'll show up tonight," Recker said.

"What makes you think so?"

"How big is this shipment, supposedly? In terms of value."

"A couple million, from what I understand."

"Think about it from your perspective. You're the boss, and you get a shipment worth a couple million dollars. Are you just gonna let it sit there for a day or two without inspecting it?"

"Good point. So the guy should be along soon."

"I would think so."

"How many men you got with you?" Recker asked.

"I got people on all sides. So once they get here, they ain't getting out. I got enough to get the job done."

"You know anything else about this from your source?"

"Not too much, really. All we know is what I told you."

"So that's your reason for rolling on this?"

"Well, that and the fact that there's this guy, who none of us knows, bringing in a multimillion dollar shipment."

"And I'm sure that doesn't sit right with Vincent," Recker said.

"You know it doesn't. Someone who's got the means to do this might have the means to set up shop permanently if we allow it."

"And you can't do that."

"No, we can't. Best way to snuff this out is to take them out before they can get settled in."

"OK. If you can wait for me, I'll be on my way."

"Good deal. What do you want us to do if things look heated before you get here?"

"If you get a chance to take this guy out, you do it. I don't need to be the one. I just want to be sure he's actually where he's supposed to be this time."

"And where's that?"

"In the ground."

11

Recker had a pep in his step as he started to get ready. He quickly explained the situation to the others.

"You really think this is it?" Jones asked.

"He used the nickname Solin," Recker replied. "That can't be a coincidence. That's where Petrović was born."

"Why would he, though? Wouldn't that be a dead giveaway?"

Recker shrugged. "Why not? Who else other than me would know that?"

"I suppose that's a fair point."

"Nobody else is going to know that's a city and not a name. If you heard that without any backstory, what would you think?"

"I would probably think it's a last name."

"Exactly. Everything fits here. The name, Eastern

European, illegal contraband, someone cunning and violent, it all fits. It all leads to Petrović. This might be the biggest thing we've had to indicate that it's him."

Jones nodded. "I can't disagree. All the signs seem to be there."

Recker looked back at his partner. "You ready?"

Haley put his pistol in his holster. "Ready to go."

"Should take about thirty minutes to get there. Hopefully they can hold out that long."

"Well, good luck," Jones said. "Happy hunting."

Recker and Haley sped out of the office. Once the door closed, Jones got up and walked over to the window, watching his partners get in one of their vehicles. For Recker's sake, he hoped they found what they were looking for.

"I hope this will be the end of it for you."

Once Recker and Haley reached the outskirts of the property, they encountered a high chain-link fence. The gate was open. Recker quickly tried calling Malloy, but he got no answer.

"Something's going on," Haley said. "I can feel it."

Recker rolled the passenger side window down. A few seconds later, there was a popping noise. Then several more.

"Looks like this is it."

"Just roll on through," Recker said.

The gunshots were an obvious giveaway that Malloy's team wasn't able to wait for them to get there. Everything was already in place. Haley gunned the vehicle, driving up to the main building. More gunshots were heard, and there was no doubt that there was a lot of activity happening inside. There were several other cars already sitting there, though none had any occupants inside.

Recker and Haley jumped out of the car and headed for what looked like the main entrance. There were lights on inside, so there wasn't a question of where they were going. When they reached the door and opened it, they instantly ducked, as bullets immediately flew in their direction.

"Get down!" Malloy yelled.

Recker and Haley both hit the floor and located Malloy's position. He was located just to their left, behind a pallet of boxes. Recker and Haley were in an open area, without much in the way of cover, so they needed to get over to his position. It was loud in there with all the gunfire.

"This place must have good acoustics," Haley said. "Can barely hear a thing outside."

"Yeah, good insulation," Recker replied.

Not wanting to stay in that spot, they quickly crawled over to Malloy. A few errant shots headed toward them, but nothing landed.

"Nice to see you made it," Malloy said.

"Guess you couldn't wait, huh?" Recker replied.

"Nope. They spotted one of our guys a few minutes ago, once the other guy got here."

"The other guy?"

Malloy shrugged. "I don't know if it's the main guy or not, but three other cars pulled up a few minutes ago. One guy definitely seemed to be in charge. Then one of my boys got spotted. All hell broke loose right after that. And here we are."

"Get a good look at the guy?"

"Nah, not really. You could tell he was the one giving the orders, though. Everyone was going up to him, he was pointing, and gyrating, and you know how it goes."

"Any of them get out?"

"No chance. They're all still here. I've still got the perimeter locked down. And all the exits are covered. Nobody's getting out of here that we don't know about. Unless we let them."

"How many are we dealing with?" Haley asked.

"I counted ten."

"Not too bad."

"They're hunkered down on the other side of the warehouse," Malloy said. "There are a bunch of crates and pallets and boxes in the way, so they got some good cover at the moment."

"You got a plan yet for smoking them out?" Recker asked.

"Honestly? I was just gonna let them keep shooting

until they ran out of ammo. They can't be packing too much."

Recker wasn't too impressed with that answer. "You ever consider that any of the pallets or boxes they're hiding behind might have guns or ammo in them?"

Malloy was silent for a moment. He almost felt embarrassed for not considering it. "Oh. Uh, yeah, I guess that could be an option."

Recker peaked his head around one of the boxes and a bullet pierced right through it, causing him to jerk his head back.

"Where's the shipment they got?"

Malloy pointed to their left, about halfway between them and their opponents, where there were several pallets of crates. They were all closed at this point, so they had no idea what was in them. Up to this point, it didn't appear that anyone was trying to escape. That buoyed the idea that whatever that shipment was, it was very valuable. They weren't going to just run and leave it behind.

"You know what's in back of them over there?" Recker asked.

"Not real sure," Malloy answered.

"If there's a door or window, that could help us."

"I'll check with who's back there." Malloy instantly got on his phone and called one of his men, putting it on speaker. "Hey, Tommy. What's the situation back there?"

"We just caught one of them trying to sneak out a door over here."

"Can you enter back there?"

"We tried, but caught a lot of resistance. We stepped back for a minute."

"All right, hold your ground. No need to get hasty." Malloy hung up, then looked at Recker. "Well, there's one fewer."

"Yeah, but we can't just sit here all day. I mean, if we know they're just wasting bullets and are gonna run out of ammo soon, then yeah, maybe. But we don't know that. For all we know they got a stack of rifles back there that'd make the military blush."

"So what's the play?"

Recker sighed. He wasn't sure he had one yet. "I don't know. We gotta figure out a way to flush them out or something. Make them move."

"Yeah, I mean, if we go rushing them, some of us are getting cut down."

Recker peeked his head around the boxes, looking at the distance between the two sides. Malloy was correct in his assessment. There were several other groups of Malloy's men scattered throughout the warehouse, and if they all charged at once, some of them wouldn't make it. It wasn't a prospect that seemed especially enticing.

"Maybe we should smoke them out," Haley said.

"That's an idea," Malloy replied.

Recker and Haley always carried a bag of things in

the trunks of their vehicles in the event they ever needed anything. It was usually out-of-the-ordinary things that weren't used on an everyday basis.

"We got one in there?" Recker asked.

"We got two," Haley answered.

Recker took another peek at the other side of the warehouse. He was still hesitant. If it got smokey in there, it'd obviously be tough to see. And they wouldn't have enough masks for everyone.

"I just wouldn't want anyone to get caught up in crossfire because they couldn't see clearly," Recker said.

"I got an idea," Malloy said.

"I'm all ears."

"If you got smoke bombs, we got control of the back door, right? We toss them in, and then make sure that door is barricaded from the outside so they can't get out. That means they'll have to come to us. We don't even have to move."

"Isn't there a window or two back there?" Haley asked.

"Smaller ones. They'd have to crawl through them. And if they do, we can cut them down as they crawl through. It'd be a perfect setup."

As Recker considered the possibilities, he knew whatever they did, there was a good chance Petrović, assuming he was there, wouldn't make it out of there alive. Part of him wanted to stand up, talk to Petrović, maybe meet him in the middle of the warehouse under a truce, and find out what happened all those years ago. And how Petrović had escaped detection for all this time. If they did what they were considering, and the smoke flushed everyone out, there was a good chance everyone on that other side would perish. And he was OK with that for the most part. But there was that piece of Recker that just wanted to find out what Petrović had been up to.

"Let's just wait a second," Recker said.

"For what?" Malloy asked. "Sounds like a good plan."

"Yeah, it is. I just wanna find out something first."

"Hey, Solin!" Recker shouted. It was hard to hear him above the gunfire, which was continuous. "Solin!"

There was no response. He couldn't be sure he was even heard above all the noise. He waited until there was a brief pause in the action.

"Solin!"

Everything went dead quiet for a moment.

"Who is this?!" Solin asked.

"Not important." Recker took another peek around the side of the boxes. "I just wanted to know what your real name is."

"It appears you already know it."

"No. I know Solin is where you were born."

There wasn't an immediate response. "How do you know this?"

"It would be the only thing that made sense. Especially if your real name is Marko Petrović. Or is it Jakov Horvat?"

"I am not familiar with those names."

Recker continued looking around the boxes, trying to get a look at who he was talking to. He kept Solin talking for a minute, trying to make out where he was. Then, he thought he got him. There was a man in a black shirt, with white writing on the sleeve. Recker could only make out part of his face, but he could see the man's mouth and jaw move as he talked. That was Solin.

Recker continued staring, trying to get a better look. But all he could see was part of the man's face. He couldn't definitively say whether it was Petrović or not.

"Maybe we should talk about how you can get out of here," Recker said.

"Maybe we should do the same for you."

Haley tugged on his partner's arm. "You know, I was just thinking. All this time we've been thinking we had them, what if the situation is actually reversed?"

"How so?" Recker asked.

"What if all this time they're just trying to keep us busy long enough for reinforcements to arrive?"

"That's a good point," Malloy said. "They could be trying to wait us out, hoping they can get up behind us. Put us between a rock and a hard place."

Recker couldn't say that was impossible. He wasn't sure it was likely, but it definitely had to be considered.

"I think you should cut this conversation short,"

Haley said. "Let's smoke them out now before we got a bigger mess on our hands."

Recker only thought about it for a couple of seconds. Haley was right. Whatever answers Recker thought he needed, it wasn't worth the possibility of an even bigger problem if they wasted any more time. They had to finish this now. If that was Petrović on the other side, all that mattered was that he didn't walk out of that warehouse again. Whatever happened before, or how he managed to stay hidden all this time, none of that was important. They were questions for another day. Right now, they just had to finish this.

"Yeah, go," Recker said. "We'll cover you on the way out."

Haley started to prepare himself. He was going to have to make a run for the door with the open space between that and where they currently were.

"Whenever you're ready," Haley said.

"Make your move. As soon as you sprint out, we'll start firing."

Haley took three deep breaths, then bolted from their position. As soon as he did, Recker and Malloy jumped up and started firing away. They were soon joined by their other men. Their adversaries instantly returned fire, but they were so busy with the men shooting at them, that Haley escaped cleanly.

Recker and Malloy took cover again, waiting for Haley to give them the word that he was good.

"Hopefully this does the trick," Malloy said.

"Yeah. We'll see."

"You don't sound so thrilled."

"I'm skeptical whether that's the guy over there that I want."

"We'll find out soon enough."

"Yeah," Recker said. "I guess we will."

12

Haley grabbed two smoke bombs out of the back of their car, and ran around to the rear of the building. Malloy's men were there to greet him. Haley noticed the two small windows.

"Make sure someone covers them if they try to escape through it."

Tommy directed several of the men to keep their eyes on that.

"What about the door?" Haley asked. "You got something to block it?"

"We got some big pieces of wood," Tommy replied. "That should be able to jam the handle so nobody can get out."

"OK. Once I throw these in, hurry up and jam that door. I don't want anyone near it in case they start firing through it to try and open it up."

"Shouldn't take long."

"Good. But if you struggle getting it in place, don't stand there trying to fix it. Forget it and move out. If they get through it, we'll just have to mow them down as they come out."

"Got it."

"All right, everybody ready?" Once he saw everyone was, he contacted Recker to make sure they were as well. After all, it was likely they were going to get most of the action from this point out. "Mike, about to send the smoke in. You guys ready?"

Recker briefly looked at Malloy, then at the rest of the men. They were all waiting. "Go ahead."

"All right. Sending it in."

Haley hurried to the door. Tommy was standing next to it and slightly opened it, allowing Haley to throw the two smoke bombs inside. Haley immediately took off, and Tommy jammed the pieces of wood against the handle. It went off without a hitch. They retreated further back, giving them plenty of room to see what was going on. They could see the smoke through the window, rising into the air.

It wasn't long until they heard some banging against the door, the men obviously trying to get out. They weren't having much luck. Then one of the small windows smashed out. A man tried crawling his way through it. One of Malloy's men instantly opened fire, gunning him down before he was even halfway through. That was the last they saw of anyone trying that exit strategy.

Now there were eight men left. As smoke filled the area, they knew they couldn't stand there any longer. Getting out through the back didn't appear to be much of an option. That only left the front. They realized that was probably a losing proposition, but it was the only chance they had.

Recker and the others readied for them. It only took a few more seconds before they started seeing some action. The men started running toward them, one by one. And one by one, they all went down.

Recker didn't even have to fire a shot yet. He let the others do that. He was saving his ammunition for the top guy. Solin. Recker looked at the bodies on the floor, and none of them were the man he was looking for.

Another batch of men tried to make their exit by running past them, but they quickly met the same fate as the others. Recker wasn't sure if any were killed trying to make it out of the back, but by judging the bodies that were in front of them, there should have only been two or three left.

He was a little surprised that the others weren't showing themselves. Unless they had some unbelievable way to get out without being seen, he wasn't sure why they hadn't appeared yet. Or maybe they had passed out from the smoke. Whatever the case was, Recker and the team weren't yet ready to check on them. They'd give it a few more minutes, just in case they were waiting for them to approach and start picking them off one at a time. They figured that was the only play those guys really had left.

With the window now open from the one man trying to escape, smoke started coming out of it. Then they heard another loud bang at the door. Solin and the other man remaining were desperately trying to get out.

"Get ready," Haley said.

Nobody back there was moving an inch. All of their eyes were focused on the door and windows. A few seconds later, there was another loud bang. This time, though, the door burst open. Two men ran out, immediately heading to their left. The first man stood there and started firing, trying to gun down a few of their adversaries. He didn't have much luck, though, as he really wasn't aiming for anyone. He was firing wildly.

He went down quickly, as he got caught with half a dozen bullets simultaneously. The other man knew it was a lost cause, and didn't try to fight. He knew that battle was over. He was just running away from the conflict. As fast and as far as he could.

There was no vehicle that anyone could see that the man was running to. He just seemed like he was moving away from everything. Maybe he was hoping he could get to the fence, then disappear once he had gotten through it. It didn't work out like he had hoped, though.

He didn't even make it halfway to the fence. At some point, he went down. One of Malloy's men, or maybe at the hands of several, had taken out his legs. The man was on the ground, clutching at his legs, as a couple of bullets had penetrated through them. He wasn't going anywhere. Both his legs had been shot, and they felt like they were on fire.

Haley, and the rest of Malloy's men, started moving in his direction. But they were being cautious. They could see that the man was still moving around, even though he hadn't gotten back up yet. And they could also see the gun in his hand, which still made him dangerous. They were giving him plenty of space.

"Not too close, boys," Tommy said.

"Keep a couple men on that door," Haley replied. "We don't know how many are still left."

Tommy then directed a couple of his men to stay by the door in case there were any more stragglers that attempted to come out. Haley, Tommy, and a couple others continued approaching the man lying on the ground.

"Try to keep him alive," Haley said. "We need to get some answers out of him."

Almost immediately after the words left Haley's lips, Solin raised his arm up and fired off a shot at one of the men approaching. With the pain he was in, he wasn't able to aim properly, and the shot missed. But it was enough to get some return fire. Two of Malloy's men opened up, putting the fatal bullets in Solin's body.

"Damn!" Haley said.

He didn't blame anyone for returning fire. He knew it was a possibility with Solin still having a gun in his hands. And judging by the condition Solin seemed to be in, getting caught and having to answer questions probably wasn't something that interested him very much.

Haley went over to the body, though he was still cautious, just in case the man had another trick up his sleeve. He kicked the pistol away from Solin's body. Then Haley knelt down and felt the man's neck. He had no pulse.

Haley stood back up. He listened for gunfire, but there was none to be heard. Everything was quiet. He looked at the men by the door, but they were just standing there. No action was needed on their part. He called his partner again.

"Hey, everything good in there?"

"Just waiting to make sure everyone's gone," Recker answered.

"Well we got three bodies out here."

Recker then counted the ones he could see. "Looks like seven on our end."

"That should be it then, shouldn't it?"

"Should be." Recker nodded to Malloy, who then motioned to his men, who immediately emerged from their positions, and started checking the rest of the warehouse. "We're checking now."

After a minute, one of Malloy's men reported back that they were good.

"Looks like that's it," Recker said.

He and Malloy got up, and they went over to the bodies on the floor, making sure they were all gone. They were. But there was still no sign of Solin.

"Meet me out back," Haley said. "Got the leader out here."

Recker and Malloy went out through the back door since the smoke was starting to dissipate. They instantly saw Haley and walked over to him. Haley immediately pointed to Solin's body.

"There he is."

"No chance at taking him alive?" Recker asked.

Haley shook his head. "He wasn't having any of that. Took his legs out. But he wasn't going to let himself be captured. Seems like he was either getting away or going down with the ship."

Recker sighed. "Some guys are like that."

Recker looked over at Solin's body, a little anxious at finding out his true identity. The body was lying face down, so he couldn't tell at the moment. But from there, it looked close. Solin seemed to have a similar build and height as Petrović. This man had a closely shaved haircut, which Petrović didn't have many years ago, but Recker already knew the hair was like this due to that glancing moment a few days prior.

"What do you think?" Haley asked.

"Could be him."

"Let's find out for sure."

Recker wiped his hands on his pants as he walked

over to the body. He was really hoping that it was Petrović, so he could put this whole thing behind him. Recker stood over the body for a moment, just staring at it. A lot of thoughts were swirling around in his head right now. He desperately wanted this man to be Petrović. And though he wished he could have talked to him, figured out what happened all those years ago, it was a moot point now. Now it was time to face the truth.

Recker knelt down, and pulled the body over onto its back. A rush of adrenaline came over him, hopeful he was about to put all of this behind him. He stared at Solin's face. It was different. It wasn't the face that he remembered. And it wasn't the face that he saw the other day. The man had a similar build as the man he knew. But this wasn't Petrović. He was positive about that.

"Well?" Haley asked. "Is it him?"

Recker continued staring at the man's face. He shook his head.

"No. It's not."

"Are you sure?"

"Positive. This isn't even the guy I saw the other day."

"Well, back to the drawing board, I guess."

Recker stood up, though he still didn't take his eyes off the man's face. There was nothing familiar about it. It was nobody he ever recognized.

"I really thought it might have been him," Haley

said. "The name matched up."

Recker thought about it. Everything did match up. Maybe that was the problem.

"Yeah, it did."

"Guess we go back to the drawing board," Haley said.

"Take pictures of all these guys. I wanna find out who all these people are."

"Think one of them might lead us to Petrović?"

"That's the hope," Recker answered. "I still can't believe that this guy used Solin as a name, the city that Petrović was born in, who has the same height and build, and it's all just a coincidence. It's hard to believe that."

"I agree. You think Petrović might have used this guy as a double?"

Recker nodded. "Yeah, I think that's possible. Maybe this guy is the key we've been looking for."

"How so?"

"Unless he's as good at hiding his identity as Petrović is, we shouldn't have as hard a time at running him down. Once we find a name, the rest should fall into line. And we can figure out how he knows Petrović."

Haley started going around to the dead bodies and snapping pictures of their faces. Recker continued staring at Solin's face. He obviously wasn't Petrović. But maybe this was the break they needed to eventually find Recker's long-lost foe.

13

The team went home for the night after the warehouse incident with Solin, but Recker sent the pictures over to Jones so he could put them through the computer. Hopefully, they would get a match. Jones worked late into the night, as he often did, so he'd have some kind of answer for when the others returned.

Recker and Haley got to the office around eight, bringing Jones some coffee from the convenience store, where they picked up some breakfast sandwiches. As Recker handed Jones the steaming-hot cup, he could already tell there was an issue.

"Your face is screaming that there's a problem."

Jones didn't even try to hide it. "Oh yes. Yes, there is."

Recker's shoulders slumped, bracing himself for the news. "What is it?"

"I've run our friend Solin through the computer system."

"And? You got nothing?"

"Oh no. That's not the problem."

"Then what is?"

"The problem is that I did find him."

Recker scrunched his eyebrows together, unsure of why this seemed to be a problem. He thought that's what they were looking for. It should have been great news. He glanced at Haley, who had an equally confused look on his face.

"That's what we wanted, isn't it?"

Jones sighed. "Yes, but not the results that I got."

Recker was now a little fearful of what he was about to hear. "I have a feeling I'm going to regret asking this."

"You will."

"Why isn't it the results that we wanted?"

"Because Solin's real identity is Jakov Horvat."

Recker stared at his friend for a moment, trying to let the news sink in. "Jakov Horvat."

"Correct."

Recker didn't have any other words right now. He knew what that meant.

"Wait a minute," Haley said. "So you're telling me that Solin is actually Horvat?"

"Yes," Jones replied.

"So we thought Petrović was Horvat, who was using an alias of Solin, because it was where Petrović was born, but now it turns out that it's totally inconsequential. Because if Solin is Horvat, he's most definitely not Petrović. So all of this...?"

"Was for nothing," Recker said.

He reached his hand back, about to knock some things off the desk in frustration. He was able to control his emotions in the moment, though. He stopped short of letting his anger out. Instead, he took a deep breath and tried to calm down.

"You're sure about this?" Recker asked. "There's no doubt that Solin could be anyone else except for Horvat?"

Jones nodded, though he wished he wasn't as sure as he was. "A hundred percent. There is no doubt."

Jones then pulled up all of the information he was armed with to prove his point. He had licenses, passports, ID's, credit cards, and tons of other things. There was no mistake. Solin was Jakov Horvat.

Recker didn't want to face his friends, and walked over to the window, looking at the cars in the lot. Everything was wrong. And they didn't seem to be making any progress whatsoever.

Jones, though he hated to do so, had to bring up the possibility that everything was in error. "Mike, at the risk of sounding..."

"Crazy?"

"No. Of course not."

"In disbelief?"

Jones wanted to put it as delicately as he could. "Is

it possible that the man you saw going into that building was actually Jakov Horvat? Maybe he's got facial similarities, and it took you back to Petrović, and in the moment, you thought it actually was Petrović?"

Recker wanted to turn and vehemently argue the point, but he couldn't. Not now. How could he? There was nothing, not a single shred of evidence that pointed to Petrović being alive, other than the shenanigans at the morgue where Petrović was killed. And that's what Recker had to hang his hat on. It was the only thing he could right now.

"There are still those people killed after Petrović was identified," Recker said.

"That's true," Jones replied. "That's true."

"And I still say that's not a coincidence," Haley said. "And there's also Horvat using the name Solin. I don't think that's a coincidence either, if that's where Petrović was born."

"There are certainly things that make you wonder. But in regards to Horvat..."

"Lawson only said it fit a pattern," Recker said. "And that pattern aligned with Petrović's methods."

"Well?"

"What if Horvat was a protégé?" Haley asked. "Someone Petrović groomed in his own image. That would explain why Horvat's pattern matches Petrović's. It would also explain why he picked the name Solin."

"Petrović gave it to him," Recker said.

He looked down for a moment, trying to get everything clear in his head. Even though he was having doubts, in his heart, he knew the man he saw was not Horvat. It was Petrović. He had to put his doubts aside and trust his eyes and his instincts.

"If you think about it, this all makes perfect sense," Haley said.

"How is that?" Jones asked.

"If you're Petrović, what better way to hide all these years, than having someone who mirrors you? That's how he's done it. If anyone ever looked into his death and had questions, if they started looking for him, like we've done, you'd come across Horvat. You think it's an alias for him. Then once you dig into it, you find out it's not an alias. It's a different guy altogether. But he moves and acts like Petrović, so then you doubt yourself. You think you got on the wrong trail."

"And the name Solin?"

"Same thing. If anyone stumbles on the name, instead of it linking to Petrović, it goes back to Horvat. You think you got it all wrong. You think Petrović is still gone. He's creating almost a clone of himself, that way all inquiries go to this guy instead of himself. It's pretty smart if you think about it."

"Almost like a double."

"Exactly. So all this time, Petrović has assumed a new identity, and maybe he's using Horvat as a mouthpiece. Maybe he's in the background. Or maybe he's out in front and just using Horvat in certain situations to act like the main guy."

"That way if things go south, Petrović is still protected," Jones said.

"There you go."

"So you believe Petrović is in fact still out there?"

Haley looked at his partner. "I trust Mike. If he thinks he saw him, I believe it. Plus all that nonsense with all those people being killed who identified Petrović? That's a coverup if I ever saw one. I've seen that move a million times. I don't think this Horvat news changes anything. Other than solidifying our thoughts about Petrović."

"Michael?"

"Everything Chris said makes sense. I don't want to lead you guys in a certain direction, though, in case I'm off base with all of this."

"You're not," Haley said. "Looks clear as day to me."

"Speaking of off base, someone should contact Ms. Lawson and let her know her computer model failed," Jones said.

"It didn't fail," Recker replied. "The information was correct. Just the conclusion was wrong."

"All amounts to the same thing."

"I'll call her. But first, how are we making out on that building Petrović went into? That's still the key, I think."

"I've been digging," Jones said. "But I haven't found much that's of interest to us. On the surface, everything appears to run as it should be."

Recker stood there, seemingly in a trance. Something occurred to him. He didn't know why it didn't until now. Maybe it was because with everything else going on, it just seemed irrelevant. The look on his face wasn't lost on his partners, each of whom could tell that he was thinking about something. They'd seen that look before.

"What is it?" Jones asked.

"I was just thinking about the girl," Recker answered. "Maybe she could turn out to be the key in all this."

"What girl?"

Recker snapped his fingers. "The girl, the woman, the secretary. At the building. She straight up lied to our faces. She knew good and well that people came into the building. And she lied to our faces and said that no one did."

"That means she's in on it," Haley said.

"Not necessarily," Jones replied. "It could be she was just following the directives of a supervisor."

"That's true."

"Even if that's the case," Recker said. "That means there's a new trail. Either she's in on it, and knows exactly what's going on, or someone told her to lie to us. And if that's true, she can give us the name of who did. Because if that's what happened, then that person definitely knows what's going on."

"OK, let me see what I can find out about this woman," Jones said.

While he was doing that, Recker called Lawson.

She quickly answered, and smiled, upon seeing Recker's face on the screen.

"Hey, what's up?"

Recker could see that she was walking through a hallway. "Just wanted to touch base with you on your computer models about Petrović being Jakov Horvat."

"Oh, uh, I'm still working on it. I got sidetracked with another project."

"Well, I think you can move on."

"Why?" Lawson walked into a room. "You got something?"

"Petrović is not Horvat."

"What? How do you know?"

"I'm sending over a picture, and some information we have on him."

Lawson finally sat down at her desk. She logged into her computer and pulled up the email that Recker was sending over. She had several monitors on her desk and started pulling different things up between them.

"He looks dead," Lawson said.

"He is."

Lawson looked at the picture of Horvat. "I don't understand. The model seemed so sure."

"It was a good theory."

Lawson sighed and shook her head. "I thought we had him."

"We still might."

"How do you figure?"

"Well, everything on Horvat still only goes back nine years, right?"

"Yeah?"

"So Horvat is probably an alias for someone else. Regardless, we have a theory that Petrović has been grooming this guy the entire time. Petrović probably gave this guy the Horvat alias, making sure this guy did everything in his own image."

"Soo... why?"

"If anyone went looking for him, all they'd see is Horvat. If they did enough digging, they'd eventually see it wasn't him, and maybe they'd give up looking."

"OK, I can see that. That's smart."

"And there really weren't any pictures on Horvat to say anything else."

"So we've got to scrap everything and start over," Lawson said.

"Not necessarily. This guy, Horvat, was doing something where he was using the nickname Solin. That easily connects to Petrović."

Lawson instantly recalled the file. "That's where he was born."

"Yes. That's not a coincidence."

"Unlikely."

"So we're starting to look down some other avenues," Recker said. "Now that we have a full-fledged picture of Horvat, maybe you can run down what his actual name is. Maybe we'll find how it connects to Petrović that way."

"OK, I can do that. What are you guys working on?"

"The only other thing we got is the building that I saw Petrović go into. There's obviously something there. We haven't found out what it is yet, but we're gonna dig a little further. There's a secretary who told us nobody came in there when I clearly saw that they did."

"So she was lying."

"Yeah," Recker said. "So we have to determine whether she did so willingly, or whether she was just told to."

"Sounds like you got a plan worked out."

Recker let out a laugh. "Hasn't done any good so far, but, we'll see."

"Well, that's what the job is most of the time, right? You run down a hundred leads just so you can find that one. That one that's elusive. But then when you find it, everything falls into place. Hopefully this secretary will be that one."

Recker looked over at Jones, who was running down the information on the secretary. Recker didn't have a sense either way on whether this would be the golden ticket. He hoped. But that's all he could do.

"Yeah. Hopefully it's the one."

14

Getting information on the secretary didn't take too long for Jones. Within a few minutes, he had everything they needed.

"I have it," Jones said.

Recker and Haley went over to him.

"What are we looking at?" Recker asked, hopeful to get some dirt on the woman.

Jones had nothing on that front, though. "Ginny Parado. It appears as though we're barking up the wrong tree with her."

"No background?"

"Nothing criminal." Jones pointed to the screen. "As you can see, a parking ticket six years ago. A speeding ticket four years ago. No arrests, convictions, jail time, etcetera."

"Doesn't mean she's not involved."

"And she's probably not the one we're looking for," Haley said. "Still got that other theory in play."

Recker nodded. "Someone told her to lie to us."

"Now we just need to find out who that someone is."

"That might take more time to figure that out," Jones replied.

Recker wasn't having any of that. "No. No more time. I'm done dancing around this thing."

"What did you have in mind?"

"That secretary knows something. And she's gonna tell us."

"Michael, do you think it's a good idea to do that?"

"Why isn't it? If she knows, then she'll tell us, then we'll know. And then we'll know who we're looking for. I don't see the issue."

"I'm concerned about leaning hard on someone who isn't materially involved."

"David, I'm not planning on roughing her up. I'm just planning on having a conversation."

"In which you'll likely scare her out of her mind."

"This woman knows what's going on," Recker said. "Or she knows who does. We need answers. She can give them to us. It's as simple as that."

"I just want to make sure we're not going too hard on her, that's all."

"Look, if she's innocent, she'll come clean pretty quick. If she's got something to hide, maybe it'll take a while. But according to her record, I'd say she'll want to talk pretty quickly after we confront her."

"Got her address?" Haley asked.

Jones wrote it down and handed the paper to him, but Recker had other ideas. He didn't want to wait another eight hours until after the woman was done with work. He wanted to get it over with now.

"Let's go over there and wait for a lunch break," Recker said.

"Sounds like a plan," Haley replied.

Recker went over to the safe and pulled out a stack of bills.

"Can I ask what you're planning on doing with that?" Jones asked.

"Using the biggest incentive known to mankind," Recker answered. "Money. If she doesn't want to talk freely. I'll bribe her."

"Oh. I suppose that works."

"I guess it's that or I could beat it out of her."

Jones put a hand up. "No, no, the money's fine."

Recker took out several hundred dollars and put it in his wallet. Then he looked at his partner to see if he was ready. Once Haley confirmed that he was, the two left the office. They went downtown again, and sat on a bench across the street from the office building. The bench was a little further back, as there was a small plaza, and a few vendors in front of them, so they weren't out in plain sight. There was also a hot dog vendor directly in front of them. But they could peek around him to see the front door. Haley looked at his watch.

"Probably an hour or so until lunch."

"Assuming she's not brown-bagging it," Recker replied.

"What do you want to do in that case?"

Recker shrugged. "I dunno. Guess we'll cross that bridge when we come to it. We can either go in and talk, or just wait until she goes home."

"That'd be wasting the rest of the day."

"Let's hope she's going out, then."

"Hope this guy doesn't move anytime soon. Pretty good cover."

Recker took a look at the hot dog stand and laughed. "Pretty sure this is an all-day thing."

"The smell's making me hungry."

"Maybe you should grab a couple."

"What do you want on yours?"

"Ketchup, mustard, relish."

"Coming up."

Haley came back a minute later with their order, along with drinks, handing Recker his.

"How do you eat it loaded like that?"

"Like what?" Recker asked.

"Ketchup and mustard? Isn't that like a cardinal sin or something?"

Recker laughed. "I like to smother it."

"Seems like a waste of a good hot dog to me."

"You should try it."

"I'll just stick with the mustard."

Recker and Haley went back for seconds not too long after that. They wound up waiting about two more hours before they got eyes on Parado.

"There she is," Haley said.

They observed her walk out the front door of the building. She immediately took a left and started walking down the street. Recker and Haley instantly got up and started going in the same direction. First, they jogged across the street. They got there just in time to see her turn the corner. Once they did, they saw her crossing the street, heading to a small cafe.

Recker and Haley stood near the corner, waiting a few minutes before they made their move. They let Parado put in her order first. After another minute or two went by, they saw her sit down at an outdoor table.

"Head over?" Haley asked.

"Let's wait until she gets her food first. People are more reluctant to leave when they've got food sitting there that they've paid for."

It wasn't much longer before a plate of salad and a bowl of soup was sitting in front of Parado. Once she started digging in, that was when Recker and Haley made their move. She was paying no attention to them as they crossed the street. It looked like she was engrossed in her phone.

When they reached the table, Recker and Haley took the liberty of sitting down on opposite sides of her. Since she wasn't expecting anyone, Parado was startled. She made a slight noise as she looked up and saw the two men next to her. She instantly recognized them.

"Oh. Um. Hi."

Recker smiled. "Hi."

"Um. Is there something I can help you with? You guys came into the office the other day, right?"

"That's right. And we need some information."

"I'm sorry, I don't know anything."

"You haven't even heard what we want."

Parado shifted in her seat. She was starting to look uncomfortable. "Look, I just work there. I just do what I'm told."

"We're not here to jam you up," Haley said. "We just want the truth."

"Four men walked into that building the other day," Recker said. "I know, because I saw them. We went in there and you told us nobody came in. So we know you lied to us. We just wanna know why?"

"Look, I'm sorry, I just... I just do what I'm told."

"Someone told you to lie to us?"

Parado looked down at her food and sighed. "Who are you guys, anyway?"

"We work for a private security agency," Recker answered. "We can't give you much more than that. What we can say is that we believe that one of the men that walked into that building is a wanted fugitive wanted by several governments. He's extremely dangerous. And if he's here, we need to find him, and put him away, before he hurts somebody."

"You can help us do that," Haley said.

"You don't need to be involved, you don't need to go to court, nobody even needs to know we were here today, or that you told us anything. If you tell us what we need to know now, you'll never see us again, and it's done with right here and now. Then you can get on with your day."

"That's it?" Parado asked. "I just tell you what you want to know right now and that's it?"

"That's all you have to do," Recker said.

Parado reached down and took a bite of her salad, contemplating. Once she was done chewing, she made her decision.

"OK. What do you need to know?"

"Four men did walk into that building that day, right?" Recker asked.

Parado nodded. "Yes."

Recker reached into his pocket and removed a picture of Petrović. He held it up for her to see. "Was this one of them?"

Parado took the photo to look at it more closely. She was squinting, appearing to have trouble with it.

"He looks familiar."

"He has long hair in the picture," Recker said. "When I saw him the other day, the hair was gone. So picture him without that."

Parado put the photo on the table and put her

fingers on the side of Petrović's face, covering his hair. She was only looking at his facial features now.

"Yeah. Yeah, I think this was one of them."

Recker immediately glanced up at Haley, almost feeling a sense of vindication.

"You're sure?" Recker asked.

"Pretty sure." She handed the picture back.

"So why did you say they weren't there when we asked?"

"I was told not to."

"By who?"

"One of the guys that came in."

"The guy in the photo?" Recker asked.

Parado shook her head. "No, one of the other guys. As soon as they came in, he came up to the desk, put a hundred dollar bill on it and said 'if anybody comes in after us, we didn't just come in here'. Those were his exact words."

"What'd you say?"

"I took the money and said OK. They were kind of scary-looking."

"I bet."

"And a hundred dollars is a hundred dollars. With inflation and all, a person needs all the help they can get these days."

"Where'd they go after that?"

"They went up the steps," Parado answered. "But before they left, the one that gave me the money said 'I'll be watching'. Then I didn't see him again after that.

I guess he just wanted to make sure I'd do what they wanted me to."

"Probably. Did you hear any names or anything?"

"No. Nobody ever offered any. But they'd been there before."

Recker raised an eyebrow. "They have?"

"Yeah. They were there once last week, and another time the week before."

"Same days?"

"No, different days and times. But they were all there. All four."

"Who were they there for?"

"They didn't say specifically. They just went straight to where they needed to go."

"You have any idea where that was?" Haley asked.

"I think it was SteelMax Consulting," Parado replied.

"What makes you think that?"

"When they left the first time, a couple weeks ago, two of them were speaking in another language. I guess they assumed they were safe talking, and that I didn't know what they were saying. And, I mean, I'm not an expert or fluent or anything, but I did pick up what they were saying."

"Which was what?" Recker asked.

"The two of them were saying something about Nilson better not screw them over or something. And Max Nilson is the owner of SteelMax Consulting. So I just put two and two together."

"What language were they speaking?"

"French. I guess some of those years in high school paid off."

Recker grinned. "I guess they did. Did you over-hear anything else?"

"No, not really."

"What do you know about SteelMax?"

"Just that they do a lot of private security work. Maybe government work, too. I'm not sure. I don't really deal with them all that much. A few phone calls I redirect to them every now and then, but that's about it. They're pretty private."

"What about Nilson?" Haley asked. "You know him?"

"I mean, he'll say hi when he walks in or leaves for the day, but that's about it. I've never actually had a conversation with him."

"You know anything else about these four guys?"

"No, nothing. Don't even know a name."

They sat around a few more minutes, asking Parado a few more questions. It was clear that she had told them everything she knew, though. And that was plenty. Now, it finally seemed as if they were getting somewhere. SteelMax Consulting was the place they needed to direct all their efforts towards.

Before leaving, Recker took out his wallet, and removed some money. He handed it to Parado.

"What's this for?"

"Your time," Recker said.

Once Parado saw there was five hundred dollars there, she was a little taken aback. "Uh, I'm not sure I can take this much."

"It's fine. You've earned it as far as I'm concerned."

"Is there some type of hitch to this?"

"No. Well, maybe one thing." Recker took out one of his business cards. It was one that only had a phone number on it. Not even a name. He handed it over to her. "If you ever see those four men walk into that building again, I'd appreciate a text message to this number."

"Is that it?"

"That's it. If you see them, you text this number and say 'they're here'. That's all you have to do. Nothing else. They come in, walk past you, and once you're in the clear, you text the number. Then put the phone down and go on with your day."

"And you'll never need me for anything else?"

Recker shook his head. "Nope. That's it. You think you can do that?"

"Uh, yeah. Yeah, I can do that."

Recker smiled. "Good." He and Haley got up. "Enjoy the rest of your lunch."

As they walked away from the table, there seemed to be a renewed energy between them.

"Seems like we might have found something here," Haley said. "That went as well as could be expected."

Recker agreed. "Yeah. Looks like we're finally on

the right track. Now we gotta dig into SteelMax and find out what they're hiding."

"Gotta be something."

"Oh, it's something all right. It's something. Just a question of what. But between us and Lawson, we'll find it. I'm sure of that. If there's something there, we'll find it. We're getting closer."

15

As soon as they had the word on SteelMax Consulting and Max Nilson, it was all hands on deck. Recker immediately forwarded the information to Lawson, and he called Jones to get him started, as well. By the time Recker and Haley got back to the office, Jones already had the rundown waiting for them.

"What do you got?" Recker asked as soon as he walked in. He was anxious.

Jones almost hated being the one to relay the news. "I'm sure what I'm about to tell you is not what you were hoping for."

Recker's mood was instantly deflated. He could feel the negativity coming. "What is it?"

"Max Nilson, at least on the surface, appears to be a fine citizen. Never been arrested, no criminal investigations against him, nothing that I can find to be a red flag anywhere."

"Except for Parado telling us this."

"Except for that," Jones said.

"Unless she was just giving us a name to get us out of there," Haley said.

"It didn't feel like that," Recker replied. "I thought she was being honest."

"Maybe she's a good liar."

"Well, Nilson's name did come up already when we ran the initial checks," Jones said. "Nothing came up then. And nothing is coming up now."

"That doesn't mean he's not involved."

"No, it doesn't. It could just mean he's very careful."

"Or very good at hiding in the shadows," Recker said.

As they were talking, Recker's phone rang. It was Lawson. She had news of her own.

"Hey, so I just so happened to have some free time over the last half hour."

Recker knew that was unlikely. Nobody at the agency had free time. There was always something going on. You just learned to shuffle projects around depending on the urgency level.

"Free time, huh?"

Lawson chuckled. "Something like that. So when you messaged me about SteelMax, I did a brief check."

"So did we. Nothing interesting."

"On SteelMax, no. But did you run Nilson?"

Recker glanced at Jones, wondering if maybe they'd missed something. "Uh, yeah, but nothing popped up."

"I don't mean the usual background stuff. He's supposedly clean on that end."

"What do you mean, supposedly?"

"Well, I already did some digging on his passport. And did you know he goes to Europe for one week every month?"

"Really? That's interesting. Nothing really criminal about it, though."

"No, but he also never visits the same place twice. Twelve different cities in the last year."

Recker still wasn't seeing the connection to anything unusual. A lot of business executives, or wealthy people, took monthly vacations. And he would have found it more odd if they were all to the same place, unless he had a vacation home in France or something.

"I can tell by your silence that you have some doubts," Lawson said.

"Well, I mean, I feel like we're kind of just throwing straws into the air here."

"We're not. Follow me. In the last twelve months, Nilson has not visited one city that would be considered a tourist attraction. You know what's on his list of vacation cities?"

"I have a feeling the Eiffel Tower is not on the list."

Lawson laughed. "No. No, it's not. Here's the list of the last twelve countries he's visited. South Africa, Egypt, Russia, Ukraine, Serbia, the DRC, Mongolia, Belarus, Kazakhstan, Uzbekistan, Turkey, and Bulgaria."

"And you don't think he was just going to those places to unwind?"

"Doubtful. In most cases, he was only there for three or four days. At most a week."

"Could have just been business meetings. He's a security consultant, right?"

"That he is."

"Do we know who he's been meeting?" Recker asked.

"No. But every single one of those places is under surveillance for various reasons. They are all hotbeds right now."

"But, again, he is a security consultant, right?"

"Why are you continuously trying to poo-poo this? I'm trying to help you."

"I know. And I'm grateful. I'm just trying to... avoid getting my hopes up too high if it's not warranted. I mean, we're flush in theories. Not much in actual facts."

"I'm not done," Lawson said.

"Oh. Continue."

"In nine of those locations, a major incident went down just after he left."

"What do you define as a major incident?"

"Terrorist activity, some type of violent incident against government or police officials, and in a few cases, we got word of major gun shipments going down, usually after they already went down."

"And with him gone."

"Exactly."

"So I get the feeling that you're trying to tell me that you think Nilson is involved with gun trafficking to these places."

"Is that the feeling I'm giving you?"

"Yeah, it is."

"Well, you'd be right," Lawson said. "I believe that's exactly what he's doing."

Recker thought about it for a moment. "That would mean he's gotta have some warehouses nearby."

"Whether that's here or over there somewhere, yeah. I'm not sure it'd make sense to have a warehouse here that you continually have to ship overseas."

"I guess that would depend on where he's getting the guns initially."

"True."

"Or, maybe he's got multiple places."

"This is mostly just speculation, though, isn't it?" Recker asked. "Not to be an ass, but that's kind of what we were doing with Horvat. And we see how that turned out."

"I grant you it's still kind of flimsy. But if you're starting to put the pieces together…?"

"What would he be doing here? He's got an office in Philadelphia for the last couple years."

"You know that these guys have to keep up with appearances. You need to have an actual business address. You have to go through with all the motions to make it seem like everything you're doing is legit. Any deviation, anything that makes someone think it doesn't pass the smell test, and you're gonna start bringing down the heat. If he's got no physical address, and he does all these things that make you wonder, eventually, he's gonna get questioned."

"But who's gonna question a guy with a small office in Philadelphia?"

"Exactly. And think about it. He's got access to several ports along the east coast if he's doing shipping from here."

"The secretary told us that Petrović and his four friends have been there for the past three weeks."

"That tells you all you need to know," Lawson said. "Something's going on."

Recker let out a sigh, trying to figure out their next moves. "Nilson isn't currently being investigated by anyone?"

"Not yet." She could hear Recker making noises with his mouth. "What's up? Something on your mind?"

"Just figuring out how to do this. Petrović isn't likely to slip up here. He hasn't in the last nine years. It's not likely that he will now. So, finding him would appear to be a longshot."

"Yeah, maybe."

"So maybe Nilson's the key to finding him. If we hook onto Nilson, if he's been dealing with Petrović, one would assume we might find them together at some point. Right?"

"Assuming their business hasn't been concluded. And you might need to do it soon."

"Why's that?" Recker asked.

"Well, if the last year serves as a pattern, he's scheduled to leave in a few days, here."

"So we gotta hurry this up."

"I wouldn't hurry too much. You don't wanna go in there and make a mistake with this bunch just because you want to get to the bottom of this quickly."

"I know."

"If history is a guide, Nilson will be back in a week or so, even if he leaves."

"Yeah, but will Petrović still be here?"

Lawson didn't have an answer for that question. They both knew it was possible that once Nilson left, his business with Petrović would be concluded. And that would likely be the last Recker would ever see of the man again. If they were going to figure out what was going on, and wrap this up, they had to do it quickly. That meant doing things a little faster than they normally would. That would mean acting without all the information up front. It wasn't how Recker normally liked to roll. But sometimes it just had to be done.

Once he was done with Lawson, Recker turned to his friends and started laying things out. He knew there would be some objections. Especially from Jones. There always was. But he also knew there weren't many options in the time frame they were looking at. He repeated all the information that Lawson gave him.

"So I think we've got several options here," Recker said. "One, we do nothing else except the track we're on. See what develops. Two, we put the pressure on Nilson. We go in there, confront him, tell him we know what's going on, see how it shakes out from there. Three, we go up to him, tell him we're looking to buy."

Jones rubbed his forehead. As usual, he had reservations. Haley also was thinking, stroking his chin, though he wasn't pondering the drawbacks. He was just thinking about the best way to approach it.

After a minute, Jones finally spoke up. "Well, I am not in favor of rushing into this. It's happening much too fast."

Recker wasn't surprised to hear it. He would've been more surprised if his partner had a different take. Haley was still silent, looking like he hadn't yet come to a conclusion.

"Chris?" Recker asked.

"I'm not in favor of maintaining the status quo. We're not gonna find Petrović the way we've been going. He's got too much of a head start and we don't know where to look outside of that office building."

"I agree there."

"So that means if we want to put an end to this, we've gotta up the pressure."

"How?"

"By not being reckless," Jones said, answering for his colleague.

"I say we march in there and confront him," Haley said. "Put him on the defensive. Any other way and we're just dancing around it."

Recker was on board. "What about posing as buyers?"

Haley shook his head. "Takes too long. If we march into that office and pretend to be buyers, he's gonna be taken aback, anyway. Then he's gonna have to vet us. He's not going to just show us a stash of weapons. And that still won't lead us to Petrović. That's taking us on a completely different path. If Nilson's business with Petrović isn't done yet, then we need to throw a wrench into things so we can be there when they meet next."

"Assuming there is such a time," Jones said.

"Petrović hasn't been there the last three weeks just for giggles," Recker said. "There's a purpose. Maybe it has something to do with Nilson's next trip."

"Why would Petrović need to show up here for that, though? With today's technologies? Phone call, video chat, messages?"

Recker looked at his friend like he was crazy. "You of all people are asking that question?"

Jones quickly realized the error of his ways. "You're right. All of those options can be hacked and traced."

"Face-to-face meeting. It's old school. But it's effective. You don't have to worry about who's watching or listening."

Jones nodded, knowing his thoughts were falling on deaf ears, like they usually were. "Well, I still have my reservations, but I know you will not heed them."

"I'm listening," Recker said.

Jones chuckled. "Yes. You're listening. But you won't do it."

"I just think my way is better."

"As you always do."

"Don't you want to put this matter behind us as quickly as possible?"

"Within reason, yes. If it's safe to do so, and we're not taking risks."

"We're gonna do it safely," Recker said.

"Oh really? By barging into his office?"

Recker grinned. "Well, I don't know if we're gonna barge in. Maybe we'll knock first."

"How reassuring. What about waiting for a text from Ms. Parado?"

Recker shrugged it off. "Waiting for something that may never come. There's no guarantee Petrović is stepping into that building again. But if we go in there and push it... we can make something happen."

Jones put his hands up, submitting to his partner's wishes, regardless of his reservations. "If you think that is the best course of action."

"Right now, that's where we're at. We've gotta make one domino fall. That's the key to this. One domino's gotta go down. Just one."

16

Much to Jones' objections, Recker and Haley went over to the office building anyway. With Nilson likely leaving in a few days, which seemed to be his usual habit, they knew they didn't have time to waste. They had to make things happen now. If it weren't for Nilson's monthly European trips, they probably would have sat back a few days. They would have tailed him, put him under surveillance, and tried to understand everything he was doing. But in this case, they just didn't feel like they had enough time for that.

So that led them to this option. Barging right in and confronting the man, letting them know they were on to him. It was a dangerous strategy, and could definitely backfire, as there was no way of knowing exactly how Nilson would respond. He could be calm and deny everything and continue on like nothing was wrong. Or he could blow up, and try to eliminate them as soon as possible. Or he could do something else that was completely unexpected. There was just no way to tell yet. They'd have to be ready for anything.

Once they got to the building, Recker and Haley devised a strategy once they got into Nilson's office. Recker would do most of the talking. That would leave Haley free to focus on Nilson's movements. They were going in under the assumption that Nilson was a shifty type of guy. That would mean he was capable of anything. That included having a gun under the desk, or a panic button that might alert guards nearby, or something else that was unforeseen. And if both Recker and Haley were focused on Nilson's words, they might not be as focused on his movements, and miss something.

When they walked into the office, they immediately got a weird look from Parado, who was sitting behind her desk. She wasn't sure why they were there. Recker gave her a smile and put his hand up to ease her confusion.

"Don't worry. We know the way up there."

Parado returned the smile, though she still didn't know what was happening. As they walked past her and started up the steps, she watched them until they were no longer in view. She scratched the top of her head as she looked down at her work again.

"Did I miss something?"

Once Recker and Haley reached the sixth floor, they found the office for SteelMax Consulting without too much trouble. At the door, they saw some type of card reader on the side. Recker tried the handle of the door, but it was locked. This was a business where nobody was getting in that wasn't invited.

"Knock?" Haley asked.

Recker shrugged. "I guess."

Recker closed his fist and knocked forcefully several times. They then listened. They heard some moving around in the office. Recker knocked again, a little more softly this time, though still loud enough to let whoever was in there know they weren't leaving. Nobody answered yet, though. But that wasn't deterring Recker and Haley. They weren't moving until somebody did. After all, they were on the sixth floor. Somebody would have to come out eventually, unless they had some web-shooters and could crawl down the other side.

Though they still heard someone moving around, there was nobody answering the door. But Recker was not going to move until that door opened.

"Try breaking it down?" Haley asked.

"I don't think we need to go that far." Recker took a step back to get a better look at the door. "Not sure we could, anyway. That looks pretty solid."

Recker was going to continue standing there, all day if he had to. But then he knocked one more time.

"Mr. Nilson, maintenance. We're cleaning all the vents today."

Whether that did the trick, or whether Nilson was

coming to the door anyway, they couldn't say. But a few moments later, the door unlocked and opened. It only opened a crack, but that was all Recker and Haley needed. They seized the opportunity, and rushed inside, pushing the door open all the way.

Nilson took a few steps back, shocked at what was happening. "Hey, what's going on?!"

The door automatically closed. Recker kept his eyes on Nilson, while Haley started looking around, making sure they were alone. It wasn't a big office. The room they were in seemed to serve as Nilson's main office. There was a closet to the side, and a bathroom, and then another large room that served as a meeting room. It had a long rectangular table with a bunch of chairs around it, and a big screen television at the end of it on the wall. Nobody else was there.

"We're clear," Haley said.

Nilson was stationary as he waited for the men to explain what they were doing there. He was a big man, barrel-chested, in his late forties. He wasn't intimidated by the men breaking in, though he was concerned about their sudden appearance.

"Who are you guys?" Nilson asked. "What do you want? You're breaking in here without permission or authority."

"Save it for the courtroom," Recker replied.

"The question still remains."

"We have some questions for you."

"I'm all ears."

Nilson casually walked over to his desk and sat down.

"Keep your hands on the desk," Haley said. He was wary of a button being pushed underneath the desk, or a gun hidden in a drawer.

Nilson gave him a sarcastic-looking smile as he complied with the directive. He then looked back at Recker.

"Now, what is this about?"

"We know who you are and what you're doing," Recker answered.

"Of course. My name is Max Nilson and I'm a security consultant. That's not a secret."

"No, you're an international arms dealer using this office as a front to conduct your business. And we know those monthly business trips you make overseas are really to meet with potential customers."

Nilson looked at him stone-faced, not an inch of flesh moving on his face. After a few seconds, he then let out a small laugh.

"You must be joking."

"Do I look like the kind of guy that jokes to you?" Recker asked.

That sarcastic-looking grin formed on Nilson's face again. "You must be. Because that is absurd."

"Is it?" Recker didn't want to dance around too long. He was just going to come out with it. "Then how else do you explain meeting with a guy like Marko Petrović? You know, someone who staged his death nine years ago and is suddenly alive, and coming into and out of this office for the last three weeks?"

The stone-faced look returned on Nilson. He wasn't quite sure how to respond at first.

"Who?"

Recker smirked. "You're gonna go that route, are you?"

"What route?"

"So you don't know who Marko Petrović is? That's what you're telling me?"

"I don't believe I've had the pleasure of making his acquaintance."

"You haven't, huh?"

"The name is unfamiliar."

"What about Jakov Horvat? You know him?"

Nilson curled his lips and made a face like he was thinking about it, though he was obviously not, and just going through the motions. He scratched above his lip as if he were pondering it further.

"I'm afraid that name isn't familiar either. Do you have any others you'd like to share?"

"Sure. How about Solin?"

"Solin? Let's see." Nilson stroked his chin. "No. I don't believe I've ever heard that one either. This is fun. Should we keep going?"

Recker smiled. He could see this would be a challenge. He was up for it, though.

"No, I think we both can see how this is going."

"Too bad," Nilson said. "I thought we were just

getting started. Well, if that's all, you know where the door is. Let it hit you on the way out."

Recker and Haley didn't move. They weren't done yet. They weren't going to play Nilson's games.

"So what are those monthly trips about?" Recker asked.

"Vacations. People do them, you know."

"Every month?"

"Is it my fault I'm wealthy enough to do it?"

"Really? I'm gonna mention some places off the top of my head. I want to know if they seem familiar to you. You ready?"

"Oh yes. I'm quite ready."

Recker looked up for a second as he remembered the names. "Let's see... South Africa, Egypt, Russia, Ukraine, Serbia, the DRC, Mongolia, Belarus, Kazakhstan, Uzbekistan, Turkey, and Bulgaria. Did I get them all?"

Nilson shrugged. "I don't know. Did you?"

"See, those were all the places you visited over the last twelve months."

"I believe that's an invasion of privacy. Are you authorized to look into my personal information?"

"Now, forgive me if I've gotten this all wrong, but which of the places I just mentioned seem like big vacation spots?"

Nilson grinned. "I like to visit off-the-wall locations. I get to avoid the crowds."

"I'm sure you do."

"And by what authority do you have looking into my personal records? That, along with barging in here, is a serious crime. Whatever you think you have on me won't stick, I can promise you that."

"Oh, did we give you the impression that we're some type of law enforcement? Because we're not."

"Who are you, then?"

"I don't think that's really relevant," Recker answered. "Plus, now you'll have to do a lot of searching to figure out who we are."

"I'm not sure you realize what you're getting yourself into here."

"I do. I really do."

Nilson started moving his right hand slightly. He put his left hand on his face, hoping that would distract them long enough to put his right hand underneath the desk. It didn't work, though.

"That's far enough with that right hand," Haley said. "Put it back where it was."

Nilson sighed, but put his hands back on the desk.

"Whatever you think you're looking for, I'm afraid I can't help you."

"I already told you what I'm looking for," Recker said. "Marko Petrović. We're old friends."

"I highly doubt that, but even if I knew this Petrović fellow you speak of, I would have no idea how to contact him on your behalf."

"Well, is he scheduled to come back in here?"

"I don't even know who you're referring to," Nilson replied.

"You're gonna die on that hill, aren't you?"

"I can assure you, whatever you think is going on here, is the complete opposite."

"So the complete opposite would be you're giving away millions of dollars to charity and your overseas trips are humanity missions?"

"Yes, something like that."

"Do I look like an idiot to you?" Recker asked.

"You look misguided."

"I know you don't know me. But let me give you some advice. I don't mind staying here all day. I've got nowhere else I need to be. And I'm not in the government or the police, so the rules really don't apply to me. So if you ever want to walk out that door again, the only chance you have is by coming clean and saying something honest and truthful for a change."

"I'm not going to say anything that will incriminate me."

"Who's asking you to? All I want to know is about Marko Petrović. Or whatever name he is using now. That's it. As soon as I have that, I'm gone. Do you understand?"

"Marko Petrović, huh? Sounds like you have some kind of personal vendetta against him or something."

"Something like that. So you can sit there and deny that he's been there until you're blue in the face, but I know different. I saw with my own eyes that he walked into this building a few days ago. I know he was here. I've shown his picture around and got confirmation he was here. And I've got word from several people that he was here to see you. And if that's not enough, I've received word that he used your name once he walked out of the building the last time. Now, you can add all that up if you want, and it all comes down to the same thing. He was here. And he was here to see you. Now, would you like to try and refute that?"

Nilson was silent for a moment. He was studying Recker's face. Nilson considered himself to be a good judge of character. And at reading body language. The vibe he was getting from Recker was that he was not a man to be messed with. And while he didn't really want to reveal any secrets, he also could see that he was not in control of this situation. If he wanted any chance of getting out of it, he was going to have to part with some information that he didn't want to.

"What assurances can you give me?"

"What assurances do you want?" Recker asked.

"That whatever you think I'm doing, or not doing, goes no further than what's discussed in this room."

That seemed agreeable to Recker. "OK. You got it."

"I'll give you straight answers on one name and one name only."

"One name's all I'm interested in."

"Before we get into all that, I need to know who I'm dealing with."

"I told you, names aren't important."

"I need a name," Nilson said. "Or you can just kill me now without getting a thing that you want."

"People call me The Silencer. That's the only name you're getting."

That was enough. Nilson's eyes jumped out of its sockets. He now knew there were no games to be played here. The Silencer was a name everyone in the city knew. Nilson rubbed the sides of his mouth as he thought about how to proceed.

"Your reputation precedes you."

Recker wasn't particularly flattered. "Nice."

"So you have a reputation of being very tough, but also very fair."

"Depends on the circumstances, I guess."

"I just want to make sure that I'll be walking out of here after you do. Because you also have a reputation for a pile of bodies being around you after you leave."

"I have no interest in killing you right now," Recker said. "I don't know much about you other than you're the one that can get me closer to Petrović. Right now, that's all that concerns me. I can't guarantee in six months that the FBI or CIA might not be knocking at your door. But if they are, it's got nothing to do with me. Because that's not how I operate. I need Petrović. And if I have to make a deal with you to accomplish that, then that's what I'm willing to do."

Nilson seemed satisfied with the response. "Sounds fair enough. I have your word, then, that you won't put me on the government's radar."

"What makes you think you're not on it already?"

"They're not already here."

"I'll give you my word from here on out, as long as you don't get in my way, no government agency will learn about your activities from me. But after we leave here, if I see you again, or you try to stop me, or I see you with Petrović, or you tip him off that I'm coming, all bets are off."

Nilson smiled and slightly raised his hands. "Sounds delightful. We have a deal, then?"

Recker briefly glanced at Haley, who wasn't taking his eyes off Nilson. Recker then turned back to the man behind the desk.

"We have a deal. You spill on Petrović, and you get to leave here in one piece."

17

Recker waited with bated breath to hear the words straight from the horse's mouth. Nilson was the man that could finally definitively say once and for all that Petrović really was alive. He just needed to hear those words.

"So… Marko Petrović?"

Nilson took a deep breath before continuing. "Marko Petrović. First, before I say anything about him, do you happen to know anything about a warehouse incident involving a man named Jakov Horvat?"

"I may have some knowledge about it."

"It was you, wasn't it?"

"Wasn't just me," Recker said. "But I was there."

"It now makes more sense."

"Was that your deal?"

"Perhaps."

Recker was starting to grow impatient. "Petrović?"

"Marko Petrović. Yes, I know him. I don't know him as... I refer to him by a different name these days, but yes, I believe that's what he used to be called."

Recker glanced at Haley upon hearing the confirmation. "What name's he going under these days?"

"Ivan Hadzic."

Recker took out the picture he had of Petrović and showed it to Nilson.

"This him?"

Nilson leaned forward and quickly confirmed that it was. "Yes."

"How long have you been doing business with him?"

"Oh, I've known Ivan for ten or twelve years now."

"So you were already aware of who he was?"

Nilson nodded. "Yes."

"I take it you've been doing business with him for all this time?"

"Off and on, yes."

"What's he doing here?"

"Working on a deal."

"With who?"

"That I cannot tell you," Nilson answered. "I do not have information regarding his business arrangements."

"What's it got to do with you, then?"

"He comes to me with an order, I help secure it for him. And provide logistics as to where it's going."

"Where's this one going?" Recker asked.

"We haven't gotten that far yet."

"When are you supposed to meet him next?"

"Undetermined. He calls me when he's ready. We have no prearranged times or places. And now that one of my warehouses is... let's just say inoperable, that makes things more difficult."

"Why are you here?"

Nilson looked at him like he didn't understand the question. "Pardon?"

"You. Why did you set up shop here?"

"Oh. Well that's easy. I grew up here. I was born in Europe, but my family moved here when I was three. So this is home to me."

"And I assume you have warehouses all over the world?"

Nilson grinned. "We agreed on one name and one name only."

"So we did. So where can I find Petrović? Or Hadzic?"

Nilson shrugged. "Couldn't tell you. I really don't know."

"You've known the guy for ten or twelve years, and you don't know how to get in touch with him? You really think I'm that stupid?"

"And you know that Ivan is a very intelligent man. That's how he's stayed alive, and hidden, all of these years. Do you think he takes any chances or risks in telling anyone, even people he's known a long time, on where he'll be at any given moment? He changes phones and addresses like most people change their socks. That's how he stays ahead. Not even I know where he is. That's how he likes it. When he's ready to do business, he contacts me."

"So you're saying you just fly around in the dark until he contacts you? What if you have something ready for him? You just wait?"

"As hard as that may seem to believe... yes. I grant you, we usually have an agreed upon time frame on things. I'll tell him something may take four or five days, so that's when he'll contact me. Not before."

Recker was still a little skeptical, but he also knew it was possible. Petrović was always a very careful man. And Nilson was right. Petrović hadn't stayed alive all of these years by being reckless or stupid. He could see how it was possible that Petrović was still playing his cards close to his chest. But that also didn't make their jobs any easier.

"So how do we find him?"

Nilson smirked. "I guess that would be like hitting the lottery for you, wouldn't it? If only it were that easy."

"Well, I suppose we could just wait here with you until he calls again. That's an option, isn't it?"

"I think that would be rather uncomfortable for all of us. I mean, I don't plan on hearing from him for at least a week or so."

"What about your next planned vacation?" Recker asked.

"On hold as of now. Your little excursion into my warehouse has put a small, but not insignificant dent into my plans at the moment."

Recker smiled. "Sorry about that. But speaking of that, how did Horvat figure into all of this?"

"Your guess is as good as mine. He worked with Ivan. He was one of his men. I didn't know him all that well."

"He used the nickname Solin. What was that about?"

Nilson threw his hands up. "Again, your guess is as good as mine. None of that mattered to me in the slightest."

"How many people does Petrović have working for him right now?"

"Couldn't tell you. I mostly only deal with Ivan. How he conducts or runs his business away from me is not of my concern."

"You don't seem to have many answers, do you?"

Nilson smiled. "Ivan is a very secretive man. If you know him, none of this would be surprising to you. Speaking of which, what is your connection to him? Why do you want him so bad?"

Recker glared at him for a second, but he had no appetite for divulging why Petrović was so interesting to him. It wasn't Nilson's business. And he really didn't want Nilson telling Petrović that he was looking for him, not that it would be much of a surprise considering they locked eyes on each other already.

"What else can you tell us about him?" Recker asked.

Nilson appeared to give it some thought for a few seconds. But he didn't have anything else.

"I think I've told you all that I can."

"So that's it, huh?" Recker said.

"As far as I can tell. I've upheld my end of the deal. I've confirmed for you that Ivan is still alive. What more can I do?"

"You can tell us where to find him, for starters."

"I can't tell you what I don't know."

"So you've said."

Their attention was suddenly diverted when they heard a noise at the door. They heard a buzzing sound, then the door unlocked. Recker briefly looked at Nilson, wondering what was going on, though Nilson looked as surprised as they were.

The door opened, with two men walking in. The first one was of no consequence. They didn't recognize him. But the second man? Recker's eyes lit up at the sight of him. It was Petrović.

"Marko," Recker said.

Petrović's eyes almost exploded out of his head at seeing his former adversary again. He immediately pushed the other man forward towards Recker to give himself more time to escape. Recker briefly tangled with the man, but he had absolutely no interest in getting into any kind of a scrape with him. Recker just pushed him aside as he ran out the door after Petrović. Haley ran out the door after his friend.

The two men ran down the hallway, chasing after Petrović, who hit the stairwell. Recker seemed to pick up some speed as they scurried down the steps. He was going full-blast in hopes of catching up to Petrović. As they rushed down each floor, Recker could see a glimpse of the back of Petrović as he turned the corner on the steps.

They seemed to be making up some ground as they raced to the bottom of the steps. Recker thought they were going to catch their fleeing target. Once they reached the ground floor, Recker and Haley burst through the door that led from the stairs to the main hallway. They temporarily lost Petrović.

Then they looked to their right and saw Petrović heading toward the exit door that led to the back of the building. Recker and Haley picked up the pace and sped after him. After a few moments, they noticed Petrović dashing out the glass door that led outside. Recker and Haley were only a few seconds behind.

Once Recker and Haley darted out the door, they saw Petrović jumping into the back seat of a black sedan that had its windows tinted. They ran after it, but the car floored it, squealing its tires, quickly speeding off. Recker pulled out his gun and pointed it at the fleeing vehicle, about to fire off a few rounds at it, but decided against it. The car was moving too fast, and was already a good distance away. Considering it was the middle of the day, Recker didn't want any errant shots to hit some unsuspecting bystander, or go through a wall or a window.

He cursed to himself and made a motion as he put his gun away. He looked around, making sure there was no one else around that was part of Petrović's crew. Maybe one was left behind hoping to catch them by surprise. They didn't see anyone, though.

"Dammit," Recker said. "That might've been our best shot at him. He just walked right into our laps. And he got away."

"All hope's not lost. We can put David on it. Check traffic cams. One's bound to pick him up somewhere."

"Yeah, maybe."

"One thing we know for sure. At least he's still around. We know that much."

"Yeah, but after this, for how much longer? He might take this as a sign to get out of here as quickly as possible. Forget about whatever he's working on."

"Even so, we can pick him up somewhere. We'll get him."

Recker wasn't as positive. The good feeling he had, of at least confirming the fact that Petrović really was still alive, had now been replaced by a sinking feeling of letting the man get away.

"Let's get back up there and have another go at Nilson," Recker said.

"Think there's more that he can share?"

"I'm positive about it. I'm not buying the 'I don't

know anything' routine. He knows more. He knows the guy for ten years and all he's got is Petrović calls whenever he needs me? I don't buy it."

"Let's get up there, then," Haley said.

The two walked back into the building, and headed straight for the sixth floor again. Once there, they ran into the same problem as before. The door was locked. Recker knocked, but they had no illusions that Nilson was going to answer this time.

As he continued knocking, Haley's eyes glanced down at the floor to the left of them. It looked like a credit card lying on the floor, partially leaning up against the wall. He went over to it and picked it up. It wasn't a credit card, though. It looked like it might have been a security card to unlock the door.

"Looks like one of them might have dropped this on the way out," Haley said.

He swiped the card into the reader, and they heard the door unlock. They put their hands on their guns, just in case they weren't welcomed when they walked in. Once the door opened and they stepped inside, they didn't see a sign of anybody. They instantly looked through the office, but there was nobody around. Nilson was gone. So was the other guy that Petrović pushed into the room.

"Looks like they took off in a hurry," Haley said.

Recker nodded and sighed. "Yeah. Another dead end. I have a feeling that's the last we've seen of Mr. Nilson here, too."

"Yeah, probably. Let's take a look around. Maybe they left something behind that's interesting."

They were hoping for a laptop or a computer, or maybe a tablet. Something that they could scrape some data off of. Unfortunately, there was none of that to be found.

"I know I saw a laptop on the desk when Nilson was sitting there," Haley said.

"Probably took it with him when he ran out of here," Recker replied.

They went through the desk, but there was nothing there of note. And there really wasn't much else in the office to begin with. That computer was probably the golden ticket. But it was gone like everything else was.

"Guess that's it," Haley said.

"Yeah. Let's get out of here and see if David can pick up on anything."

They walked out of the office and immediately went back down to the first floor. Once they got to the front desk, they stopped to talk to Parado.

"Did you see Nilson come down here?" Recker asked.

"Yeah, he went flying out of here with another guy."

"One of the guys that came in with that group of four?"

Parado nodded. "Yeah, he was one of them. They ran out of here like their hair was on fire or something."

"Did you see which way they went after they left?"

"No, I'm sorry."

"It's OK. Thanks."

Recker and Haley walked outside, and instantly spun their heads in each direction, hoping Nilson was out there somewhere. They knew it wasn't likely, though. While they were chasing Petrović, Nilson had enough time to be a few blocks away by now.

"Well, I'd say we accomplished something here today," Haley said. "We shook some things loose from the tree."

Recker had his hands on his hips. He should've been happy that they finally had confirmation of what he suspected. Petrović was alive. There was no doubt in anyone's mind. He was alive. But instead, he couldn't help but feel disappointed. Petrović was right in his grasp. He was only a few feet away. But he couldn't reel him in. Now, Petrović was out there again. Only now, he knew Recker was looking for him. That changed the game somewhat. If it wasn't already challenging enough, it would be even more so now.

"Let's get back to the office," Recker said.

"We'll come up with something. We'll find him again."

Recker wasn't as sure. But he hoped that was the case. This was where Petrović excelled. Blending in and escaping. They found him once. But he wasn't sure they could do it again. Hopefully Petrović wouldn't become a ghost for the second time.

18

Recker and Haley rushed back to the office, filling Jones in before they got there. They wanted their partner to get a head start on finding Petrović and Nilson while they were on the way. When Recker and Haley finally reached the office, there was only one thing on their minds.

"How are we looking?" Recker asked. "Find either of them yet?"

Jones continued typing and didn't take his eyes off his work. "It's still a work in progress."

"A traffic cam should've picked them up."

"Yes, well, I didn't see the car, so I can only run it through the facial rec software at the moment. And so far, Petrović's face is not turning up."

"And it won't," Haley said. "He got in the back seat. Tinted windows."

That was not a deterrent, though. Jones immediately put his finger up, having another plan. He moved his chair to the left to another computer and brought up a different screen.

"You two come here," Jones said. "You know what the car looked like." There was a map on the screen, to which he started pointing at. "This is a map of the area. It's an interactive map I've created. It also has all known traffic cameras." There were camera icons on the map to signify the locations on the lights. "Now, all you have to do is click on one of those icons, and it'll bring up everything it's captured. So you know the car you're looking for and the relative time. All you have to do is find it."

Recker and Haley instantly sat down and started going through the footage.

"While you're looking for that car, I'll keep on Mr. Nilson," Jones said. "Do you think the two will be meeting up again soon?"

"If Nilson's to be believed and they've known each other as long as they say, I'd put good money on it," Recker said. "They're going to want to try and regroup. The warehouse incident put a kink in their plans. They've got a few men dead, and some weapons, and money, they can no longer count on. Now this is making them scramble. We're a wild card that they weren't expecting."

"They're gonna have to resurface somewhere," Haley replied. "Especially if they've already got something in the works, and it appears that they do, they can't just sit underground until all of this blows over. They got deadlines they've gotta meet."

Recker agreed. "So they should come back up for air soon. It's just a matter of being there when they do."

Recker and Haley continued going through camera footage, looking for the black car. The one thing they had going for them was that they had an exact time to sort through. That made it a lot easier than looking for a random car with no idea when or if it came through a certain area. They at least had that going for them.

After looking through a few different camera locations, they finally stumbled on one that fit. Haley almost jumped out of his seat as he saw the car on the screen. He quickly pointed at it.

"What's that?"

Recker zoomed in on the vehicle. "Looks like that's it." They studied the car further. "Tinted windows."

"That's it."

Recker continued on, stopping the screen again once the car had turned. It gave a nice picture of the license plate. Recker zoomed in again, then wrote down the plate number.

"Twenty-to-one that comes up as stolen."

Recker shook his head. "No bet."

He would have been shocked if the plate actually led to that car. It would have been a rookie mistake. One that he didn't believe Petrović would make. He would've bet everything he owned that it was a stolen car. He then pulled up another tab and entered the license plate number.

"So that comes back to a..." Recker looked at the make of the car. "Yeah, that's not it. Definitely stolen."

They went back to the camera screen and tried to pick the car up at other spots based on where they assumed the car was traveling.

"Perhaps it would have been prudent to go to Nilson's home address to see if he turned up there," Jones said.

Recker turned his head to look at his partner. "I wanted to get back here with what we had so we could try and find the car."

"We may have missed an opportunity with Nilson in the process."

"I assumed Nilson wouldn't go straight home."

"You know what they say with assumptions."

"Yeah, but I'm also assuming that he's got other contingencies in place in case of something like this happening."

"You could be right," Jones replied. "You don't think it'd be wise to head over there now, do you? In the event he might still be there?"

"I can't imagine he would be. Even if he did go there, it'd only be to get something he really needed. He'd be out of there in less than five minutes."

"Might not be a bad idea to check," Haley said. "Just in case he thinks he's safe there."

"If we showed up at the office, and we dug into

where he's been, he's gotta know we know where he lives too. He'd be an idiot to go back there, and we know that he's not."

"Still, might not hurt to check. I can head there while you guys stay here and do this. We split up, cover all the bases."

Recker thought about it for a moment. He thought it would be a waste of time, but he figured it probably wouldn't hurt, just to make sure, in the event Nilson did something unexpected. Plus, they both probably didn't need to be there at the computer looking at the same thing. It would cross more boxes off the to-do list.

"OK. If you wanna head down there, sit on the place for a while, see what develops."

"I'll give it a while," Haley said. "Nilson might think it best to wait a while before returning, wanting the heat to die down a little."

"Yeah, possible."

Haley got up to get ready to leave. "Let me know if you come up with something that you want to roll on."

"I will."

Haley then left the office, leaving Recker and Jones to continue on with their respective tasks.

"How are you making out over there?" Recker asked.

"It's tough sledding."

"Haven't found him anywhere?"

"No, that's not the problem," Jones answered. "I've found him."

Recker stopped what he was doing. "Then I don't understand. If you found him, what's the problem?"

"The problem is that I've lost him after that."

"Oh. Where'd you find him?"

"He ran into a parking garage a few blocks over from the office. Unfortunately, I haven't seen him leave."

"Well, I guess it's possible he could still be there."

"I've also seen a couple dozen cars go out of there, and the camera angles do not give a good view of the driver."

"So he could have been in any one of them," Recker said.

"Or none at all."

"How big's the garage?"

"Holds several hundred cars."

It wasn't music to Recker's ears. Nilson could have had a car waiting there to meet him. Or he could have stolen one. Or he could have just been waiting for something. But going there to check it out didn't seem like it would be the best use of his time. Recker kept up with what he was doing, trying to find the car that Petrović escaped in.

"It must feel good to you to know that you were right," Jones said.

"I'll feel good when I find him again."

"Still, you had doubts about what you saw. It turns out your instincts were correct."

"I guess so. Hey, I've got the plate number of this

car. Can we just plug that number into the system and have it pull up whatever camera has spotted it?"

Jones gave him a disapproving look and shook his head. "Did you really just ask that?"

Recker shrugged. "What?"

"Of course we can plug the number in. Who do you think you're dealing with?"

Recker smiled. "Just making sure."

Jones rolled his chair over and pulled down a few boxes from the top tabs, typing the number in that Recker had written down. Within seconds, a host of red dots suddenly appeared on the screen.

"And there we have it."

Recker's eyes scattered across the screen, seeing a couple dozen red dots. "What exactly am I looking at? What time frame?"

"These are all the places that a camera has picked up that license plate today."

"So everything on the screen is just today?"

"That's correct."

"OK. Not too bad. Can we filter it to put them in order to where it first got picked up today until the last time?"

"Seriously? You're asking me if it's possible?"

"Well I assume it's possible, knowing you. But I don't know how to do it."

"Watch and learn," Jones said. A few more buttons, and there was a small number hovering over the red dots. "Voilà."

"OK. And how do I change the dates?"

Jones then showed him how. "Do you have something in mind?"

"Well, looking at the screen for today, both the first time the plate was picked up, and the last time, up to now... they're both in the same general area."

"Thinking that's where he's living?"

"Maybe," Recker answered. "Can't really draw up any conclusions based on this. Obviously too small of a sample size."

"So you're going to expand it?"

Recker nodded. "That's what I'm going to do. Using this plate, if they've been using it for a while, we should be able to get a clearer picture of everywhere it's been in the last few weeks."

"And using that, we can start to draw some conclusions on where they might be heading next?"

Recker grinned. "Now you're learning. Hopefully we'll be able to get an area where Petrović is staying. Then we can start to hone in on it. But even if we don't, if we can figure out the places he's going..."

Recker never finished his thought. He and Jones were already on the same wavelength. Jones went back to his computer.

"It appears I've trained you well."

"The student has become the master," Recker said.

"Well, I don't know if I would go that far. Once you have that nailed down, I can start checking motels, and hotels, in the area. See if I can latch onto anything."

"Don't think that'd do much good."

"Why not?"

"I can't see Petrović staying in a hotel around here."

"Again, why not?"

"I don't think he would trust it. A lot of eyes. Cameras. I think he'd be wary of being spotted somehow."

"So where would he go?"

Recker scratched the side of his face as he thought about it. "I think he'd be more likely to rent a place out for a month. Someone who's got a condo available, an Airbnb, something like that."

Jones saw the logic in that. "It would probably make more logistical sense for him."

"Avoids a lot more hassle."

Using the tools that Jones showed him, Recker then changed the dates on the screen, going back to the first time that the license plate was picked up by a camera. That turned out to be four weeks ago. And there were a lot of red dots on the screen, all over the area. The dots were mostly concentrated in the greater Philadelphia area, though there were some instances of it being picked up in New Jersey, New York, Delaware, and even Maryland. But there was no doubt the heaviest part was located in the Philadelphia area. That's what Recker was going to concentrate on now.

Recker's eyes lit up upon seeing how many dots were on the screen. There were a ton. It seemed as if Petrović had been a pretty busy man lately, at least as far as his travels went. Recker immediately started trying to connect things together.

Jones glanced over at him. Recker looked almost overwhelmed by what was on the screen. "How are things looking on your end?"

"Looks like... I've got a lot of work to do."

"Do you need help?"

"No, you just continue on with Nilson. I'll keep on with Petrović."

"Hopefully that will give us something."

"Let's hope," Recker said. "If there's a pattern in here somewhere, I'll find it. I'll find it. And then, I'll find him."

19

The team didn't break it up the previous night until well after one in the morning. And they were back at it early, with Recker and Haley both returning just a little after seven. They weren't surprised to see Jones already hard at work.

"Did you even sleep at all?" Recker asked.

"I got a few hours in," Jones answered. As soon as he said it, he stretched his eyes open a little more.

Recker and Haley immediately went to the coffee machine, hoping it would help to wake them up. As they started drinking, Jones swiveled his chair around to face them. He had a somewhat smug look on his face. The kind that a person had when they knew something when everyone else in the room was in the dark. It wasn't lost on his partners. Recker brought his cup up to his lips and stopped as he looked at his friend, wondering what his issue was.

"Why do you look like that?" Recker asked.

"I've found something."

Recker instantly put the cup down. "You found him?"

Jones put his finger in the air. "I did not say that. I said I found something. I didn't say I found him."

"Close enough."

Jones then pointed to the large screen on the wall where he was about to present. "See here."

Recker and Haley moved around to face the screen. They saw a map appear, with what looked like several places circled.

"What are we looking at?" Recker asked.

"Based on what you found last night in regards to the places Petrović's car was most frequently spotted, I did a search of the surrounding businesses in those areas."

"What'd you find?"

"A boatload. I'm erasing everything on the screen, and circling the greater area. Based on the patterns, Petrović is most frequently in this area. So I did a search to see if he might possibly be living in this vicinity."

"Come up with anything?" Haley asked.

"Not in terms of that. Mostly because this is basically an industrial area."

"Doesn't mean he couldn't be living there," Recker said.

"Correct."

Jones then circled a bunch of buildings that were on the screen as he continued his presentation. "So then I started digging into businesses and buildings. Going under the assumption, and I know it is only that, since this is an industrial area, that perhaps this area represents the place he most frequently is doing business."

Recker stared at the map, which was only an aerial view of. There were three buildings circled.

"I'm assuming there's something special about these three?"

"Indeed there are," Jones replied. "Knowing what our friends are into, and considering we already found one warehouse with weapons in it, I'm going under the assumption that perhaps that is not the only one."

"I'd say that's a good assumption," Haley said.

"So with that in mind, I did some research into all the warehouse buildings in this area. I checked to see what warehouses have been recently leased in the last six months. There are only a few. So I checked on who owns those buildings, as well as the person who signed the lease, and what businesses are currently operating out of them."

"Is that these three?"

"No."

"Then how do they fit in?"

"I'm getting to that," Jones answered.

"This year?" Recker joked.

Jones basically ignored him. "In any case, in all of

those instances, everything checked out. There were no anomalies or red flags in regards to anything."

"Maybe expand the timeline. Six months isn't necessarily the starting point. We know that Nilson's been here a long time."

Jones rolled his eyes. "Of course. I am getting to that."

"Oh, OK. I just wasn't sure if I should go home and take a nap first."

"You're more impatient when you're tired."

"I hadn't noticed. So back to these buildings."

"Hopefully," Recker said. "I just had three more birthdays and Petrović has moved six times since we started this conversation."

Jones chose to ignore him again, only shaking his head. "As I was saying, back to these buildings. I expanded the timeline from six months to a year. That once again proved to be pointless."

"Are we going to go back a decade?"

"My, my, someone really is cranky this morning."

"No, I would really just like to speed things up a bit. I mean, it's not like Petrović is on any kind of schedule or anything. I'm sure he's just waiting around for us to show up somewhere."

"Can the sarcasm wait until at least noon to show up? Please?"

"But then the morning would be so boring," Recker replied.

Jones took a deep breath, not wanting to engage in

the debate any longer. "Anyway, back to these buildings."

"Oh, good."

"I expanded the search back to two years."

"Are we going to go back to the Reagan administration?"

Jones now had his comments on ignore. "So I went back two years. And I found several buildings that fit the parameters I was looking for."

"They were dusty?"

Jones gritted his teeth. "To cut things short..."

"Finally."

"Should I just give up? Hmm?"

Recker finally let out a smile. "No, I'm done. Proceed with your lecture, Professor. I mean, we have all day."

"I'm just going to give up and let you figure it out."

"No, no, I'm done. Really. Go ahead."

Jones hesitated for a moment, waiting to be interrupted with another sarcastic comment. There was none coming, though. He had a feeling if he continued on for too long, however, that more barbs would be thrown his way. He really did want to cut it short now.

"So long story short...," Jones waited for a comment.

He and Recker looked at each other, both waiting for the other to say something. Recker knew what his partner was waiting for. But it wasn't coming. Recker just gave him a grin.

"Basically, these three buildings are all owned by one man."

Recker put his hand on his chin as he looked at the map. "Let me take a wild stab at this. Max Nilson?"

"Incorrect."

Recker scrunched his eyebrows together and shot his friend a look. He didn't see how he could be wrong.

"Incorrect? You're not gonna tell me it's owned by Petrović, are you?"

"No," Jones replied. "Any more guesses?"

"David."

"OK, OK. The buildings are all in the name of Madison Brewer."

"Who the hell is that?"

"If you'll let me finish, I'll tell you. Madison Brewer is one of Nilson's ex-wives."

"One of?" Haley asked. "How many's he got?"

"Three. She's number two."

"They divorced several years ago. These buildings were part of the divorce settlement."

"So how does she figure into all this?" Recker asked.

"She doesn't even live in the area," Jones said. "She resides in Texas. Houston to be specific."

"So is she involved? Does she know what's going on?"

"Difficult to say right now."

"So it looks like those three buildings are a good place to start," Haley said.

"I'd say one of them is a good place to start."

"What? Why? What's so special about one?"

Jones erased everything and circled the one building he was talking about. "This building here is the only one of the three that's supposedly vacant."

"Supposedly?"

"Well, it wouldn't be vacant if it's got guns or other illegal things in it."

"True."

"The other two buildings are leased out, and from what I can tell, rather legitimate businesses. I've found nothing alarming about them. But that third building, just sitting there empty."

"Makes sense," Recker said.

"Oh, I'm so glad you approve of my hypothesis."

"So Petrović could be making deals, and this warehouse could be where his supply is."

"That is my theory."

"Sounds like a good one," Haley said. "Seems like this is the next step for us."

"Anything else we know about this place?" Recker asked.

"It has not been used for any legitimate business for over two years. And that is a long time for a place to go unused."

Recker stared at the map. "It certainly is."

"What about where Petrović might be staying, like we talked about?"

Jones lifted a cheekbone, having nothing good to

report on that front. "I've found nothing even close to being interesting. Like we said, if he's using an Airbnb or something, we're not going to locate him that way. He's undoubtedly using a fake name, anyway. I've done a preliminary search on all hotel and motel computer databases, trying to match up when someone has checked in, but there's not much there." Jones then circled the building on the screen a few more times. "I believe this is our best bet right now."

Haley was on board. "Looks like a winner to me."

Recker looked at his partners and nodded. "I agree. So let's get after it."

20

A fter Recker and Haley got ready, they bolted from the office and immediately went to the address in question. It was located in an industrial area, with a bunch of other warehouses and factories around. It was at the end of a dead-end street, with the warehouse having a chain-link fence and gate to enter. There was only one way in.

They sat in the middle of the street, in the parking lot of a neighboring building, sizing up their options. They didn't really like the situation as it presented itself.

"One way in," Haley said. "Not all of these places have gates and fences. Wish the one we needed didn't."

Recker stared at the fence. "Look at that fence and gate. Doesn't look old and rusted. No holes in it. Not like you usually see with older places where nobody's doing business."

"Someone's taking care of it. Making sure nobody gets in that's not supposed to be there."

Recker took note of the top of the fence. At least as far as he could see. A little further down the line in both directions, some trees got in the way to block his sight. He didn't notice any cameras. But that didn't mean someone wasn't watching. The cameras might have been hidden, or in another location. It was obvious this was not going to be the way they got in.

"You wanna just sit and wait or do you wanna push it?" Haley asked.

Recker glanced at him for a second. He wasn't quite sure. He didn't want to rush into anything before they had a full grasp of the situation. And he wasn't sure they did, yet.

"Let's pull up the map of this place, see what we're dealing with."

Recker got on a tablet and pulled up a map of the area. There was a wooded area to the back of the warehouse. There didn't appear to be anything else behind it. Not even a road. Not for a while, anyway. There were other buildings to the side of the one they were looking at, separate roads leading into them.

"Well, if we decide to break into this thing, we're gonna have to do it from the back."

"I agree," Haley said.

"If we don't, the only other thing is just waiting here to see who goes in or out."

"We might not notice if it's Petrović that's going in,

though. Depending on the amount of cars, and whether he's blocked from our view or not."

"I don't know if we can take any chances of being seen going into this thing. If someone goes in, and closes the gate, we'll probably have to plow through it. That'll give them time to get ready for us."

"But there doesn't appear to be an escape route other than the entrance."

"True. But if people go in, and Petrović isn't there, we might blow ever finding him again."

"There's gonna be some risk to whatever we decide," Haley said.

Recker nodded. There was no doubt of that. "I say we wait. At least for a little while. Even if it's only a day. There's no reason for them to think this place has been compromised. And even if they do, they're not going to leave all that merchandise in there, assuming there is some, and they haven't had enough time to get rid of all it if they close up shop and go somewhere else."

"So we'll wait."

"For now. We'll see how long that lasts."

"You know, there's another thing we gotta think about."

"What's that?" Recker asked.

"Now Nilson's on the move. Petrović knows we're coming. They both might be running scared. That could mean they up their plans and do whatever they were doing sooner. Or they could change them alto-gether. What if they were planning on coming back here, but now with us in the picture, they just decide it's not worth the chance and they're already in Mexico?"

Though Recker didn't want to believe that was the case, he had to admit that it was possible.

"We'll just have to see how things develop here. With as much product and money on the line, I have a hard time believing they'd just walk away from it. You know as well as I do the power of greed."

"We're assuming there's money and product in that building," Haley said. "Doesn't mean there is, though."

Recker sighed. "Yeah. Not sure what other options we have at the moment, though. Like I said before, we just have to hope that they haven't had enough time to close shop yet. I fully believe that's what they're probably intending now. But if that's the case, that would probably mean they'll be along pretty soon. They'll wanna close things out soon so they can get out of here. But I just can't believe they'd leave anything valuable behind."

"Assuming there is anything."

"Yeah. Assuming there is anything."

Recker continued talking and throwing different theories into the air for the next couple of hours. That was all they had to go on. Nobody had showed up, and they weren't ready to break into the place yet. They were going to try to give it as much time as they could. They were in almost constant communication with Jones, who was also trying to do what he could to find

Petrović or Nilson. Jones put alerts out for if or when Nilson used one of his credit cards, passports, or half a dozen other items that could be tracked. So far, everything was coming up empty.

While they were waiting, Recker and Haley were also on their tablets, looking for any kind of information that might help them in locating their subjects in the event they never showed up there. At the three-hour mark, they finally got a visitor. Haley peeked up and saw a car driving by. He quickly tapped his partner on the arm.

"Looks like we got business."

"Just one car," Recker said. "Tinted windows, of course."

They observed a man get out of the sedan, walk over to the gate, and put a key in to unlock the padlock. Once the chain was off, he opened the gates and the car drove on through. The man then closed the gates and put the chain back around the gate and locked it.

"We could cut that off with some bolt cutters," Haley said.

"Let's give it more time. Besides, I doubt they're doing anything with that car. If they've got product to move, they're gonna need a truck. Or a van, at least."

"Yeah, that's true. They're not gonna move pallets of guns, or drugs, or whatever else they got with that small car."

"They could just be the advance team. They come, check everything out, make sure everything's good to go. Then when they give the word, the rest of the team comes."

"That would make sense. No use in putting everyone in danger right away."

"Let's just see where this leads," Recker said. "I think it confirms there's something in there, though."

"How you figure?"

"Who would come check on an empty building?"

"If they don't leave relatively soon, I'm going to assume someone else is coming."

"And if they do leave soon?" Haley asked.

"Then I still assume someone else is coming. Especially if they're not leaving with a trailer hitched to their car, or it's not weighted down like they're leaving with more than they came with. This has gotta be the scout party. Petrović often did that when I was tracking him. When he wasn't sure about something, he sent someone else in first to assess the danger. If he got the word everything was good, then he'd show up."

"Could be following the same principles here, then."

"Tigers don't usually change their stripes. Alter them, maybe. But not change them."

They sat there looking at the building, though they lost sight of the car. They could see the front of the building from where they were, but the car drove around to the side, where they could no longer see from their vantage point. A half hour passed. There was no sign of the car leaving, and nobody else went in.

"What are you thinking?" Haley asked.

"I'm thinking business is going to pick up soon. Be ready. Nobody needs to spend thirty minutes in a building that's empty. If they were just doing a routine check, they'd be out by now. They're waiting for something."

Haley heard something and looked to his right, seeing a truck driving down the street. "Could be this."

Recker looked over as the 26-foot long box trucks drove in their direction. "Yeah, I'd say that's about what I was looking for."

"Looks like you can fit a good amount of cargo in that."

"Illegal cargo."

"That too."

There were no markings on the truck. The cab, as well as the rest of it, was just plain white. Not a single thing on it. As it drove past them, it stopped as it waited at the gate. Haley grabbed a picture of the license plate. He immediately sent it to Jones.

"Need all you can get on this ASAP."

The truck waited there, idling, as it waited for the gate to open. After a minute or two, the driver honked the horn. Then, they saw a man running toward the gate. It was the same person that got out of the sedan and unlocked it before. Once the gate was open, the truck drove on through, with the other man locking things back up again.

Recker and Haley continued watching as the truck drove up to the warehouse, then turned around and reversed. They saw one of the bay doors on the warehouse open as the truck backed up. With the distance they were at, it was hard to see anything of note, but Recker thought he saw a pallet or two with boxes on it.

Both Recker and Haley grabbed their guns and started getting ready, making sure they were locked and loaded. Recker glanced back up at the truck, which was still backing in.

"Looks like maybe it's time to spoil the party," Haley said.

"No time like the present."

21

As Recker and Haley stared at the truck, they began making plans.

"Straight ahead?" Haley asked. "If we go around to the back, that leaves it wide open up front. Don't know who or what's going on."

Recker nodded. He didn't like the idea of splitting up, but he disliked the idea of not having any eyes out here knowing what was going on. For all they knew, by the time they rolled around to the back, five more cars could've driven up. Or, they could get around to the back only to find out their targets had already left. No, one of them had to stay there.

"I guess I'll head around to the back," Recker said. "You keep an eye out here."

"Sounds good."

Just as Recker was about to get out of the car, he

glanced over at the truck again. It had stopped, as it successfully backed into its spot. They heard the back door lift up. Then they saw a man get out of the truck. There was no one else in it, unless there were some that were already hiding in the cargo area.

Once the driver was out, the man from the front gate went over to him and they started talking. It seemed like a cordial discussion. But Recker still didn't get out of the car. Haley noticed his partner was hesitating.

"Something wrong?"

Recker couldn't put his finger on it yet. "No, not really."

"Well something seems wrong."

"This just seems off."

"Off? In what way?"

"I don't know. Like, maybe this isn't the time to strike."

"Why not? What are you thinking?"

Recker didn't take his eyes off the driver as he continued talking to the other man. "Only one car came in. Plus this truck."

"Right?"

"Nobody else in that truck except the driver. We couldn't see in the car, except for this guy at the gate."

"Yeah?"

"Doesn't seem like now's not the time to go in there. Petrović isn't there."

"How do you know?" Haley asked.

"Do you really think Petrović would come here with only three other guys? I mean, unless there's more hiding in that truck, or he was in the back of that car, I don't get the feeling Petrović would come here unless he had an army with him."

"Yeah, you might be right. You know him better than I do."

"I just feel like if Petrović was there, he'd have at least twenty other men there with him. That way if something went wrong, there'd be enough of a distraction where he could get away. Or he could eliminate the problem. Either way."

"So what does only three men being there say to you?"

"That he either expects a problem, and he's offering these three up on a silver platter if there is, or…"

"Or what?"

"Or he's waiting somewhere else."

"What's your gut say?"

"My gut says he's waiting for these guys to bring that truck somewhere else," Recker answered. "He's not sure if there's a problem. If there is, he'll let these guys take the fall for it. If there's not, then he'll be waiting elsewhere."

"Could be. What do you wanna do here, then?"

"Let's just wait it out. Maybe some others will show,

who knows? But if not, if this is all there is, I say we wait."

Haley was good with that. "One thing's for sure. If that truck gets loaded up, it's gotta go somewhere."

Recker nodded. "And we'll be there wherever it goes."

"Even if we're wrong, and Petrović really is in there somehow, he's still likely going wherever that truck goes."

"Yeah. But if we go in there and wipe everything out, Petrović is going to assume we're on to everything. I doubt he would return to any place he's got anything stashed in. He'll just move on. It's not worth the risk right now. Not until we have a better handle on things."

Haley then made a video call to Jones, wondering about that truck. "David, you got anything on that truck yet?"

"The truck is legally registered to one of the businesses owned by Madison Brewer. One of those other buildings we talked about."

"Maybe it's headed back to one of them after this?"

"It's possible, though I don't know how likely it is at this point."

"Why not?"

"I did a quick scan of the license plate to see if any cameras have picked it up anywhere this morning," Jones replied.

"And?"

"It did, though not in the areas of those other businesses. It came from a different direction."

"Where?" Recker asked.

"That, I have not been able to decipher yet. I haven't pinned down the origin. I just know it was the opposite direction of those two other buildings."

"So there's a good chance it's not going back there."

"A good chance? I don't know. A chance? Yes."

"Speaking in riddles."

"I don't know where it's going or where it came from. It's registered to Brewer in the name of one of the other businesses. My guess? And it's only a guess, I'd say it's going to some other place that we don't know about yet."

"At least that's something," Haley said.

"Not much," Recker said. "But something."

"I'll keep working on it, see what I can run down," Jones replied. "How much time do you think you have?"

"Oh, all day. You know, take your time."

"Sarcasm will get you nowhere, Michael."

Recker smiled. "Probably not. No, just do what you can do. We're gonna follow this thing regardless, so even if you can't pin it down, we'll figure it out once we get there."

"Assuming you don't lose the tail."

"When was the last time I lost a tail? Especially a big truck."

"There's a first time for everything."

"Yeah, maybe so, but I'm not losing this truck. Not even if I have to hop on the top of it and hold on for dear life. I'm not losing it. This could be our last and best shot to find Petrović. We gotta make this work."

"OK, I'll keep working on it and see if I can come up with something."

They continued staring at the activity by the warehouse, though by this point, all they were looking at was the truck. The two men had gone inside.

"You know, it'd be a shame if the police got an anonymous tip right about now," Haley said.

"Yeah, it would be. Too bad it can't happen. We need to find out where that truck is going."

"Any ideas?"

Recker shook his head. "No, but the more I think about it, I have a feeling it's going somewhere that's not connected to Nilson."

"Why's that?"

"Well, if you think about it, that warehouse we found Horvat in, that was connected to Nilson. When I first saw Petrović, it was outside Nilson's office. Then we were in Nilson's office. And we almost got Petrović when he wandered in. Now this place is connected to Nilson. It's in his ex-wife's name and all, but Petrović has gotta know that if we're digging into Nilson, we'd find this place. And probably any others."

"He's gonna assume we'll be coming here soon."

"Exactly. He's not going to just transfer this stuff to another place that's connected to Nilson. Whether it's him or an ex-wife or an alias or whatever. Petrović is going to send this someplace that's clean of any ties."

"Wonder if he's already got that spot lined up."

"I don't know," Recker said. "I'd assume that if he did, it would already have been there. I mean, why take the chance of leaving the stuff here if you already had another spot?"

"Maybe because Nilson had control over things and was comfortable here?"

"Could be. I mean, it was safe here until we came along. One thing's for sure, if Petrović is involved, he's taking a more hands-on role right about now."

Nobody else showed up to help with the truck. And they felt almost certain that Petrović was not in that warehouse at the moment. Not quite an hour after getting there, they saw the driver of the truck reemerge outside. He was then joined by the other man. They talked by the front of the truck for a few minutes.

"Looks like it might be go-time," Haley said.

The one man went over to the gate to unlock it and open it. Once he did, the truck drove on through. Recker didn't pull out after it at first. They'd give the truck some room. After all, it was too big to lose them, even if they ran into traffic. When the truck got to a stop sign at a small intersection, it stopped. It was just waiting there, even though there was no other traffic.

Recker and Haley looked back at the warehouse, seeing the first car now outside the gate. The passenger was locking the gate again. The car then pulled in right behind the truck.

"Looks like they're riding shotgun. Giving the truck some protection."

Recker put the car in drive. "That's what they think. Because they're not protecting them from us."

22

R ecker and Haley followed the truck all the way onto I-95. The sedan was right behind the truck. They didn't need to follow the vehicles that closely, as the truck wasn't exactly speeding to get away from someone. And it was highly visible. There were several cars in between them. There was no chance they'd be losing it.

At first, since they were driving to the airport, they thought that might have been the destination. Perhaps they were putting the cargo on a plane for an unknown destination. But they drove right past the airport. It soon became clear that the destination was Delaware.

After driving for close to ninety minutes, the truck finally got off 95, and it was clear the trek was coming to a finish soon. They were beginning to drive down some local roads, so Recker and Haley were preparing themselves to stop in the not-too-distant future. They drove for another fifteen minutes.

Now was the really challenging point of tailing someone. It wasn't too hard to remain hidden on a major highway or busy street when there were dozens of other cars around. You just had to duck behind a car that was bigger than yours for a moment or two. But when you got off that major road and there were no other cars around? That's when it got hard.

The truck got off one of the main roads and turned down a little-used road. There were scores of trees on both sides. The sedan still followed. Recker had to slow their vehicle up a little. They just couldn't get too close now.

Once Recker's car turned, they still had the truck and sedan in sight, though it was further up the road. Recker stepped on the gas, not wanting the car to get so far ahead that they lost them. If they got made, they'd just have to deal with that. But they couldn't lose that truck. As Recker floored it, they started gaining some ground. Haley had some reservations about catching up to them so quickly.

"Mike, you might wanna hold back the reins a little bit."

"We can't lose them."

"We're gonna lose them if they see us coming and we get into a fight with them before they get to where they're going."

"Even if we do, we know they're heading somewhere around here," Recker replied.

"That's still guesswork. That'll still take some time to figure out exactly where. If we stay on this truck without getting spotted, then we'll know for sure."

"But if we lose them by hanging back, we'll wind up in the same position."

They went up a small hill, losing sight of the truck and sedan for a minute once they were on the other side of it. Recker continued pressing the gas. Once they were on the other side of the hill as well, they continued making up ground.

It appeared to be a barely traveled road, as they hadn't passed a single other car along the way. But the road seemed to stretch on for a while. Eventually, the road curved, and the truck was out of sight again. As Recker floored it once more, not wanting to lose sight of the truck for any length of time, they went around the curve as well.

Only, there was something waiting for them now. Recker slammed on the breaks, seeing a roadblock directly in front of them. They could see directly behind the roadblock, as the truck and sedan kept on driving. But now there were a couple of pickup trucks, facing each other, blocking the road. The only way Recker was getting around it was to go through them. The trees lined pretty close to the road, but maybe it was possible. Though Recker figured if he tried it, the trucks would have moved with him. Either way, they were clearly in a jam.

They appeared to be at a standstill. But it was about to get worse. Recker checked the rearview mirror, and observed several more cars driving in their direction. He didn't think it was a coincidence that all of a sudden, more cars appeared, when all this time they hadn't seen any.

"Business is about to pick up," Recker said.

Haley turned around. The cars approaching weren't driving in one single line, either. They had both lanes blocked, and it seemed like they were three deep on both sides.

"Looks like we got a situation here," Haley replied.

They were quickly surrounded, though nobody seemed to be too eager to make the first move. With vehicles blocking the roads now in both directions, a couple other cars drove on the grass to each side, effectively taking out any exit that Recker and Haley had. They were mildly surprised that no gunfire had erupted yet, though.

"Wonder what they're waiting for."

"Maybe they want a few answers first," Recker said.

That was the only explanation they could think of. They had the manpower to start blowing holes in their car right now. Of course, maybe they weren't eager to get into a battle without knowing who they were dealing with. Still, though Recker couldn't see their exact numbers yet, with eight cars there, assuming two people per car, there had to be at least sixteen. Sixteen against two. That was pretty good odds on their side.

Nobody had gotten out of their cars yet. And Recker didn't notice any guns even pointed at them so far. This sure wasn't going down the way he assumed it would. Not that he was complaining about not having to duck bullets. But it wasn't making sense to him yet.

Finally, a man from one of the cars behind them, got out of his car by the passenger door. He stood there, not taking any steps further. His door was still open, giving him a little protection in case anyone started firing at him.

"Hey in there! Looks like there's a problem."

Recker rolled down his window. "Sure does!"

"Why don't you get out and we can talk about it?"

"I'm comfortable here."

The man smirked. "Well, here's the thing, you've got nowhere to go. And you're not getting away. So you might as well just get out."

"What do you have in mind?"

"You're outgunned. By a lot. I'm not sure what your intentions are here, but that doesn't really matter to me. If we were interested in killing you, we'd have opened up by now."

"So why don't you?" Recker asked.

"Those aren't my orders."

"So what are they?"

"Give yourselves up, we take you somewhere, and then you have a little chat with someone."

"And then they kill us?"

"I'll be honest, I don't really know what the plans are after this. The fact that they don't want you dead yet implies maybe there's a chance for you. But at least you'll have one. Maybe you can talk your way free. I don't know. Like I said, I don't really know or care what happens after this. As long as I do my job here, that's all that matters to me."

Recker whispered to his partner. "Send Jones a message, let him know what's happening. Have him track the car." As Haley was doing that, Recker continued the conversation with the man outside. "So that's the plan? Take us hostage?"

"Well, we don't have to call it that. Let's just call it... willingly agreeing to come peaceably."

"And who are we going to see? Nilson? Petrović?"

"I don't think names are necessary at this point. You'll find out when you get there."

"If I'm going to meet a violent death, I'd just assume I'll make it now as opposed to later."

"Like I said, I don't know what the plans are for you. Maybe they'll try to kill you. Maybe there's something else in mind. But at least there's a chance that's not in the picture. If you do something now, you don't have one."

"I don't know about that," Recker said. "As far as I can tell, the odds are in our favor."

The man laughed. "Oh really? Looks like there's

only two of you in there. There's sixteen of us. And you think the odds are in your favor?"

"That's right."

"That's pretty funny."

"You're the only one laughing."

"I'm almost tempted to open up on you right now. Just for laughs. Just to see how good you really are."

"I'm fine with that," Recker replied.

"But like I said, that's not what my orders are. Still, if that's how you wanna play it, I guess we can oblige. Make your move whenever you want."

Recker passed Haley his phone, and his partner then opened up the glove compartment. There was another secret compartment in there, in back of that, where Haley then stashed their phones. If they were getting taken, they weren't giving their phones up. Not that they usually had much in the way of incriminating evidence, but there were some phone numbers stored. There was no use in letting their adversaries have it.

"All right, we'll play it your way," Recker said. "We'll see where this goes."

"Great. Glad to hear it. All you have to do now is throw your guns out the window. If I see anyone make a sudden move, we're just gonna open up. I don't care if you're reaching for a gun, a hanky, or a piece of gum. It don't matter to us."

"Understood."

Recker and Haley then tossed their main guns out

of their respective windows. Then they did the same with their backup weapons.

"That's it," Recker said.

"Fine. Come out now. Slowly."

Recker and Haley opened their doors, and instantly put their hands up. The men surrounding them slowly walked toward them. They all had guns pointed at the two men. Once they were surrounded, both Recker and Haley had their hands tied behind their backs. They were going nowhere.

The man in charge then got on his phone and made a call. "Everything's good here."

"So what now?" Recker asked.

"You're about to find out."

Everyone started looking beyond where the two pickups were. Someone got behind the wheel of one of them and moved it slightly onto the grass. Recker and Haley kept staring in that direction, assuming that someone was coming. Their assumption wasn't wrong. Not even a minute later, they noticed a car driving towards them. It was a black sedan. Tinted windows. It was driving at a normal speed.

Recker thought he had a good idea about who was in there. There could really only be two options. Petrović. Or Nilson. Or maybe the two of them together. There was really no other option that he could think of. There was no doubt in his mind it was one of them. He was a little anxious about which one of them it would be.

The car got there in almost no time at all, parking around where the pickup truck had vacated. Recker's eyes were glued to the vehicle as he waited for someone to get out. He didn't think they were just bringing in a different car to transport them somewhere. They could've done that with the vehicles that were already there. No, this was definitely someone higher up who wanted to meet face-to-face.

Once the car stopped, there was a notable tension in the air. Nobody got out at first, though. With the windows tinted, Recker couldn't see inside. But he knew he'd find out who it was soon enough.

Finally, the back door opened on the passenger side. Someone was getting out. At first, the back of the man's head was to Recker. He could tell it wasn't Nilson. Not unless the man got a closely shaved haircut in the last few hours. Then the man turned around and started walking toward the prisoners. Recker's eyes locked onto him. It was Petrović.

Recker's blood started to boil. He was this close to Petrović. After all these years thinking that the man was dead, and now seeing him up close and personal again, he just wanted to attack. Petrović had a stoic expression on his face as he approached Recker and Haley. He obviously recognized Recker, and anticipated meeting him again after their last two encounters, though one was only at a brief distance.

Petrović stopped a few feet in front of them, though he was really only focused on Recker. He had no history with Haley, so he really was of no consequence to him. Recker and Petrović stared at each other. It was a little surreal that after all these years they were within an arm's distance of each other again.

"We meet again. I must say I never thought I would. Well, until the other day when you saw me going into that building. Then I believed it. I knew. One day. We would have this moment again."

"How are you still alive?" Recker asked.

Petrović laughed. "Planning. Careful planning. Once you showed up the last time, I knew you were not going to let go. So we put things into motion."

"What are you doing here?"

"I could ask you the same thing."

"I'm looking for you."

Petrović continued laughing. "Well, it looks as though you found me, doesn't it?"

"Seems like it."

"Only it appears like the circumstances are much different this time around, huh?"

"For now."

Petrović smiled. "It is what I always admired about you. Even when you were chasing me, I admired you. Respected you. Still do. You're relentless. When you're in pursuit of something, you don't let go. You can't. It's like an itch that you cannot scratch. It's not that you won't let go. You just can't. I appreciate that tenacity."

"How about you let me go and I can show you some more of it?"

The smile didn't fade from Petrović's face. "I'm glad to see the years have been kind to you. They haven't beaten you down like they do some men. You're the same man I knew all those years ago. It'd be a shame if we found each other again and you were some broken down shell of a man, blubbering all over himself or something like some people are."

"Glad I didn't disappoint."

"Great," Recker said. "So what now? You just gonna kill us?"

"No, not yet. Not yet. We have much to discuss first. There are a lot of things I want to know. But here is not the place for that."

"Oh, you have a dungeon waiting?"

Petrović laughed again. "Always the charmer. I have missed a challenger like you. You keep a man on his toes. Iron sharpens iron, right?"

"If you say so."

Petrović motioned to his men. "Put them in a car and take them away."

"What about their car?" the leader of the group asked.

"Take it with us. I don't want it sitting on the side of the road so someone can find it. And I want to have it searched in case they have anything in there we need to get rid of."

As everyone started to scatter back to their cars, a couple of the men escorted Recker and Haley to the back seat of one of them. Petrović also walked along with them.

"Sorry about the whole shooting you thing," Recker said. "Nothing personal."

Petrović smiled. "No. Nothing personal. It was just business, right? You had your job, and I had mine. It's just the way it goes for people like us. But now? Now the situation is reversed. Before, you were the hunter. You had me in your crosshairs. And you couldn't let go. Now... now I am the hunter. And you're in my sights. Like a deer in the middle of the woods with a scope pointed right at it. And there is nowhere for you to go."

23

Recker and Haley were sat down on separate chairs, though they were fairly close to each other. If it weren't for their hands being tied behind their backs, they could've reached out and touched each other. They were in the middle of a decent-sized room, though it was cold, and dark. They could still see, but there wasn't much to look at, other than the concrete floors and cinder block walls. There wasn't a single piece of furniture in the room other than the chairs they were sitting in.

After being led into the room, the men left Recker and Haley to themselves for a few minutes. But they were under no illusion as to what awaited them.

"I wonder what their plans are."

"I think we both know the answer to that," Recker replied.

"Yeah, but I wonder if they'll do it nice and slow? Or will they take the speedy route?"

"Let's hope for nice and slow. It'll give David some time to find us."

"What's he going to do?"

"He'll have to enlist Vincent's help, I'd imagine. Unless he finally feels comfortable with that bazooka."

Haley laughed. "Somehow, I doubt it."

"Me too. Whatever we do, we gotta try and hold off for as long as we can. Tell them anything if it'll buy us some time. We need at least a couple hours."

"Speaking of telling them things, at least we're not gagged or blindfolded. At least we can see what's coming."

"Yeah. For now."

"Maybe that's what they're debating," Haley said. "I'm sure we're throwing a wrench into the plans."

"Yeah, I doubt this was on their bingo card for today when they woke up."

They continued to sit there, conversing with each other, whittling the time away for the next few minutes. Finally, the door to the room opened up. A sliver of light hit the room, though it was quickly blocked out by someone entering. They had a chair with them. They brought it in front of Recker and Haley, setting it down between the two of them. The man then stepped to the side. Petrović entered the room. Three other men followed him, with one of them closing the door, though they all stayed back against the wall. They were only there to observe. And if somehow one of their prisoners broke free. That didn't seem likely, though.

Petrović sat down on the chair, his gaze alternating between the two prisoners in front of him, Recker to his left, and Haley to his right. He didn't say anything at first. He had somewhat of a cocky grin on his face, believing he held all the cards here. And he probably did.

Recker was the one that was mostly of interest to Petrović. After all, he was the one Petrović had a history with. But he was still curious about Haley.

"You have the look of an agency man," Petrović said.

"Should I take that as a compliment?" Haley asked.

Petrović smiled. "If you wish."

"Then thanks. I will."

"What's your name?"

"Chris."

"Chris what?"

"Marigose."

"Sounds like it's made up."

"Not my fault who my parents were."

"Slightly more original than our mutual friend, John Smith, right John?"

Recker shrugged and tilted his head. "Not my fault that's the name the agency gave me."

"Neither of you were carrying wallets," Petrović said.

"We don't like to leave calling cards in case of capture."

"Indeed. How did you find me again? After all these years, I never thought I'd see you again."

"You weren't the only one," Recker said. "And I didn't find you."

"You saw me that morning going into Nilson's office."

"I saw you going into the building. Had no idea it was Nilson's office."

"But you still saw me."

"Complete accident."

Petrović laughed, not believing that for a second. "Oh, come now. You really expect me to believe that our eyes met by chance?"

"I don't care what you believe. That's what happened. We were just going to lunch. I happened to see you getting out of a car, and I'll be honest, for a while there, I was starting to think I was going crazy. Because, you know, it's not everyday you see someone you thought was dead."

"So you really didn't know I was alive? You really weren't here tracking me down?"

"As hard as it may seem to believe, I really wasn't. I don't work for the agency anymore. And as far as I knew, you were dead."

Petrović chuckled again. He got the sense that Recker was being honest with him.

"Imagine that. All of this, all by some fluke coincidence of us both being in the wrong spot at the right time. But if that's true, there's something about this that troubles me."

"What's that?" Recker asked.

Petrović threw his arms out wide. "Why all this? What are we doing here? Why are you following me? Looking into Nilson? Why all that if you're not still with the agency?"

Recker briefly looked up at the ceiling, trying to get his thoughts in order. "Well, it basically comes down to this. You were a job to me. And as far as I knew, that job was completed. So now, when I see you all these years later, I realize the job's not finished. And I always complete my assignments. Always."

"Even if you no longer work for the agency?"

"A job's a job. To me, the circumstances don't matter."

Petrović smirked. He didn't believe that. He knew why Recker was still after him. It was personal. Always has been.

"You and I both know differently, don't we?"

Recker shook his head. "It's just about finishing things up."

"So when you saw me, that triggered all sorts of things in that head of yours, didn't it?"

"Just an unfinished job."

Petrović snickered. "You... you're something, you know that?" He started waving his finger at Recker. "You're something. Nobody, and I mean nobody, worries about completing an assignment nine years later, for an agency they no longer supposedly work for, unless it's personal. And it is for you. Isn't it? Always has been. It's always been personal."

"Nope. Just a job. And I don't like leaving things undone."

"Nah. You might be able to snow this new partner of yours, but you and I know the truth, don't we?"

"It's just what I told you. That's it."

Petrović still had that cocky look on his face. He knew he was in complete control here.

"Well, I think there's one of two things going on here. One, you're lying, and you're still working for the agency, and you're now trying to clean things up. Or two, you're really not employed by them anymore, and then we both know what that means, don't we?"

Recker, with a look of contempt on his face, glared at him. The urge to break free from his chair and strangle Petrović with his bare hands was growing stronger by the second. He hadn't been truthful about the real reason he still wanted Petrović after all these years. While yes, there was still that mantra about always wanting to finish a job, and the fact that one apparently had gotten away still burned at him. But that wasn't the overriding reason for wanting the man so bad. Petrović was right. It was personal.

Petrović, still grinning, turned his attention to Haley again. "Do you know why your partner wants me so bad?"

"An unfinished job?"

Petrović laughed. "No. That's the story he keeps giving you, probably. But that's not why you're here. You're here because your partner, John Smith..." Petrović glanced at Recker. "That's what you're still going by these days, yeah?"

Recker didn't reply.

Petrović waved his hand. "Ah, no matter." He turned back to Haley. "Anyway, the reason your partner still has this burning hatred for me is because when he first got assigned to my case, at least as far as I know, he tried to stop me from killing someone. It was a man who had double-crossed me. He was the reason why the CIA was now on my tail. He was an informant. A rat."

"So?" Haley said.

"Well, as you can imagine, this enraged me. I cannot have men I do not trust in my midsts. So I killed him."

"Lots of people get killed in this business. Unfortunately, part of the job."

"Yes, but I had to make an example out of this man. I had to let it be known far and wide what happens when you betray my trust. It is not just to kill you. No, then I have to take extreme measures."

Haley thought he was starting to see where this was going. He winced in anticipation of what he was about to hear. But he wasn't sure exactly how far Petrović was taking it.

"The man had a wife and three small children. All under the age of ten, I believe."

Haley briefly closed his eyes, now knowing what he was about to hear.

"So unfortunately, they all had to be dealt with," Petrović said. "And in a fashion that would make everyone take notice."

Petrović glanced over at Recker, who took a deep breath, then lowered his head to look at the floor. Visions were starting to run through his mind again. Just as if he were there again.

"So therefore, the man and his wife had to be killed to send a message."

"And the kids?" Haley asked.

"Well, it would have been cruel to leave them alive without parents. Especially after I killed them in front of them."

"You killed their parents right in front of them?"

"What else could I do?"

"You sick, tormented, piece of..."

Petrović put a finger in the air, and laughed. "Ah, ah, ah. It's not nice to call names."

"What kind of person kills children?"

"The kind that does not appreciate being messed with. See, when I got word the CIA was sending someone to find me, I thought it would be appropriate for whoever that person was... that they would find what happens when someone betrays me. And then your friend John entered the picture. He went to the man's home, and found the carnage waiting for him. And yes, I had a man watching from a distance, just so I could get a picture of who it was the CIA was sending."

"So did you kill them for revenge or to send a message?" Haley asked.

"Perhaps it was a bit of both. You see, I had hoped that whoever stumbled into that scene, it would haunt them. It would enrage them. It would make them so mad that they wouldn't want to do anything else other than kill the person responsible."

"Why would you want that? Seems counterproductive."

"I thought the man that wandered into that scene... it would no longer be just a job to them. It would be personal. I mean, who finds a dead family on the floor and shrugs it off like it's no big deal, right?"

"You're a sick man."

Petrović laughed, almost finding it a compliment. "Maybe. But I'm also a smart one. How could a man see all that and not let it cloud his judgment? How could he operate as he normally would?"

"So it's all just a game to you?"

"A game of survival, yes. A normal man, one who cares about what he does, has to let that affect him. And once it does, he ceases to operate as he normally does. Instead of being elite, he becomes average. He becomes normal. And that's what happened." Petrović looked over at Recker again. "You remember those times, right John? I do."

Recker stared at him, but he had no interest in reliving those times. Not that it mattered. With everything Petrović was saying, it was coming back to Recker anyway, whether he wanted it to or not.

"See, John had an opportunity to kill me several times as I would soon find out. But he didn't take them. Remember the rage I was talking about? Instead of taking the shot as an elite-trained agent would, that would be taking the easy way out. That's taking the impersonal way out. There is a family that needs to be avenged. There is a thirst for revenge that needs to be quenched. That means getting up close and personal. Much more personal than the situation requires. That means wanting to inflict pain. Punishment. Wanting the man responsible to pay, and pay severely, for the things he's done."

Haley glanced over at his partner, who was staring straight ahead. He now understood why Recker was intent on finding Petrović again. The man wasn't just a regular execution file. It was more. It was personal. And Haley understood it.

"So I guess that leads us all here to today," Petrović said. "Which begs the question, how did you find me? And who are you working for?"

"We already told you that," Haley said. "The answer's not changing. We don't work for anybody except ourselves. And we found you by accident. Just like he said. Saw you going into that building."

"So just an unlucky accident for me then, right?"

"That's about the size of it."

"That seems rather unfortunate for me, then, doesn't it?"

"You said it."

"Unfortunately, I do not believe it. I don't believe in random, chance encounters. They don't happen."

"They do in this case," Haley replied.

"So out of all the places in the world, you two just happened to be where I am, in that exact moment and time?" Petrović shook his head, having a hard time coming to grips with that deduction. "No. It can't be."

Haley shrugged. "Suit yourself."

"Let's just pretend, on the off-chance that you're telling the truth, and you're not still with the agency, who else are you working with?"

"We work alone. Just the two of us."

"So you're telling me you have no outside help. Nobody behind the scenes."

Haley nodded. "That's right. It's just us."

"See, now I think you are lying to me."

"No, you're right. We are working with someone. As a matter of fact, you guys should get moving. Because they're about to bust in here any minute now. Then you're in trouble."

Petrović laughed again. He appreciated the man's

style and sense of humor. He still didn't believe a word of what he was hearing, though.

"Should I sound the air sirens? Get ready for the big offensive?"

"Laugh if you want to," Haley said. "You'll be the one lying on the floor when they bust through here."

"I think not. But I do think there might be other people I need to worry about."

Haley shook his head. "There's nobody else. How many times do we gotta say it?"

"Until I believe it. Which I don't."

"Not our problem."

"Oh, but it will be," Petrović said. "Because there are many means, many avenues, in which to get the truth out of somebody. If you can't get it through honest conversation, then you have to resort to other methods."

Both Recker and Haley knew what that meant. If Jones didn't get there soon, they were likely in for a long night of punishment. Not that it was likely going to prevent some torture. They didn't think Jones was going to be able to work that quickly. Especially since they were ninety minutes away. But considering they were trained in withstanding torture techniques, they'd be able to hold out longer than most people could. Of course, Petrović was well-schooled in this type of behavior as well. But nobody, no matter how tough, or how trained they were, could hold out forever. Everyone had a breaking point. They'd just have to hope Jones got there with reinforcements before they found out what theirs was.

Petrović stood up, then took a few steps back, almost analyzing his two prisoners. He pushed his chair away, then looked back at his men, who were still standing against the wall.

He motioned towards Haley. "Take him to the next room."

Two of the men walked over to Haley and helped him out of his seat. They held his arms as they led him out of the room.

"Two of us too dangerous for you?" Recker asked.

Petrović smiled. "No, not at all. But two of you together, you may try to top one another. See who can go the longest without breaking. There's strength in numbers. Neither of you may want to seem weak in the eyes of the other. Unwilling to divulge something you may be more willing to talk about without the other around."

"That's a bad plan. Neither one of us is going to talk. Doesn't matter if we're in the same room or not."

"Perhaps. We'll just see about that."

"Nothing to see. Won't happen. Take your best shot."

"Oh, don't worry about that. I will. And I don't want you to be under any illusion about what's about to take place. You're in for a long night, and a world of pain."

24

Recker was knocked off his chair for the umpteenth time. He lost count after seven. He was feeling aches and pains all over his body. His mouth, nose, jaw, cheek, forehead, stomach, all of which had been repeatedly hit over the past few hours. Of course, nothing had changed in all that time, except the amount of pain he was in. He still hadn't divulged anything that Petrović considered useful. He really didn't say much of anything at all. Both he and Haley were sticking to the script that they were only working together. There was nobody else with them.

As Recker was lying on the floor, Petrović stood over him, holding his hand. He shook it out for a second. One of his men then came over to him.

"Maybe they're telling the truth. Maybe there is no one else."

Petrović took some steps back. "Maybe. They can withstand more, though. Check the other guy."

"I just came from there. He's not saying anything either. That's what I'm saying. Maybe this is it. Let's just kill them and be done with it. If they knew anything else, or other people were with them, they'd be here by now, wouldn't they?" The man pointed to Recker. "I mean, they wouldn't let them be subjected to this, right?"

Petrović took a deep breath as he looked at Recker's lifeless body. "Maybe. Let me take a crack at the other guy first."

"And if he doesn't talk?"

"Then we'll be done with them. Then we can kill them."

About half an hour went by, and Recker could hear the faint sounds of someone screaming. It sounded like Haley. Then the sounds stopped. Still lying on the floor, he was facing the door, and could see some light under it. He saw the shadow of someone's shoes standing there. Then the door opened. Petrović led the way, followed by one of his associates.

"What's the matter Marko? Losing your touch?"

One of the men picked Recker up and put him back on the chair.

"I remember a time you used to be an expert torture specialist."

Petrović didn't look pleased at being needled. Recker could see he was hitting a nerve.

"Not used to not getting the answers you want, huh? Well, maybe that's because you're questioning grown men and not trying to beat answers out of children these days."

"Get the stick," Petrović said.

His man didn't look happy about it. "Can't we just..."

"Get the stick!"

The man quickly left the room to get the device his boss was talking about. Petrović was now planning to unleash the most amount of punishment he could on his old foe. A smile slowly returned to his face.

"You think you're going to rattle me or something? Get me to do something that will set you free?"

Recker shook his head. "Nope. I expect you to do something stupid. You always do."

The smile faded from Petrović's face again. "I don't know what you're planning here, but it's not going to work."

Now Recker was the one smiling. "It already is."

"What's that supposed to mean?"

"You're a smart guy. You figure it out."

Petrović turned his head to the door. He was starting to worry he had missed something. Then the door opened again. It wasn't who Petrović was expecting. Instead of getting what was commonly called a cattle prod, Max Nilson walked through the door.

"What are you doing here?" Petrović asked. "We weren't supposed to meet again until tomorrow."

"I heard about our friends here and came over to see what the commotion was about?"

"Heard from who? One of my men talked to you?"

"That's not important," Nilson said, waving his hand in the air as he walked past his friend and partner. "What is important is him."

"It's under control."

Nilson stopped just in front of Recker and leaned over. "Nice to see you again."

Recker grinned. "Yeah, I was hoping we would."

Before they could get any further into their conversation, Petrović grabbed hold of Nilson's arm, and pulled him over to the side of the room.

"What are you doing here?"

"Seeing how things are going," Nilson answered.

"I've got it."

"Get anything useful yet?"

"Not yet," Petrović replied. "We're working on it."

"Judging by his appearance it doesn't seem like it's going very well. Maybe he's a man that can't be broke."

"Every man can be broke. You just have to push hard enough."

"What about their car? Did you find anything in it?"

"Nothing. Completely clean."

"There's something odd about this," Nilson said.

"Like what?"

"Like why they allowed themselves to be captured.

They had to know this was what was waiting for them."

"They had to take their chances," Petrović said. "They were outnumbered. It was either fight and die or give up and hope you have a chance to free yourself later."

Nilson was unsure about that, but wasn't going to press it further. "How much longer do you intend to be here doing this? We have other matters to attend to. My office is now compromised, and we've lost two warehouses in all this. This is taking up valuable time that we should be putting in other directions."

"I need to know what he knows. I need to know how many other people are coming."

"What makes you think it's not just them?" Nilson asked.

"Just a feeling."

"Great. While you're here playing around, basing things on feelings, there's millions of dollars possibly slipping through our fingers. Get your head out of your ass and let's go. If they can't or won't tell you anything in the next thirty minutes, forget it, put a couple bullets in his head, and move on. We've got other things to do."

Petrović didn't like being talked to in that manner, but he didn't reply or get heated. He soaked it in. Maybe Nilson was right.

And Nilson wasn't done making his point. "Look, I don't care what kind of history you have with this guy.

That doesn't matter. The only thing that matters is what we've got coming up. There are millions of dollars at stake here. And the longer you stay here fooling around with this guy, the more that becomes in jeopardy. We have a lot of product to move and get to the ships. And that's not going to happen by itself. So the longer you take here, the more resources you put into this nonsense, the more we risk everything."

Petrović was taking the discussion to heart. "Thirty more minutes. If I've learned nothing by then, I'll end it."

Nilson seemed satisfied with that. "Fine." He then looked at his watch. "I'll expect to see you down at the port in three hours."

Petrović nodded. "I'll be there."

Nilson put his finger in the air, emphasizing his lack of patience. "Don't be late."

Once Nilson walked out the door, Petrović turned his attention back to Recker, who was going to try to seize the moment and goad his enemy longer.

"Looks like someone's about to be put in the time-out chair."

Petrović still had an angry look on his face. "I'm really going to enjoy these last thirty minutes I have with you. But you... you won't enjoy it so much." He looked back at the door and started walking to it. "Where is that stick?!"

As he opened the door, he heard the popping sounds that were unmistakable. There was a fight happening just outside. He then rushed to wherever the sounds were coming from. The door stayed open, allowing Recker to hear the gunfire in the background. Considering the situation, he had to assume Jones enlisted the help of Vincent, and they had finally arrived. He had lost track of the time, but he figured they'd been there around three hours.

The gunfire continued for several minutes. It always sounded like it was going on for a lot longer than it actually was. Then it suddenly stopped. That was always the hardest part, especially when you weren't directly involved in the combat. You had no idea what was happening.

About five minutes elapsed. Recker heard footsteps. It sounded like people were running. It was getting closer. Then he could tell someone was just outside the door. They were being careful. Someone peeked inside, then went in. They were followed by several more people.

"We're clear!" a man yelled.

Recker instantly recognized a couple of the men, but there was no doubt when he saw Malloy walk into the room. One of the initial men that came in went over to Recker and untied him.

"Well, well, well," Malloy said. "Never figured you for a man who just sat around and let everyone else do the fighting. Comfortable?"

Recker couldn't help but crack a smile as he stood up. He felt his stomach and ribs and winced.

"Looks like you got worked over a bit," Malloy said.

"Yeah. Chris is here."

Haley then walked through the door, looking about the same as Recker did. He had his hand on his cheek.

"Man, this might be the worst I've ever seen you two," Malloy said.

"Wanna take a picture?" Recker asked.

Malloy chuckled. "I'll pass."

"I take it David brought you here?"

"The one and only. Sorry it took so long. We had to get things together quickly and come up with a plan."

"You got here just in time as far as I'm concerned."

"What's the word on those gunshots I heard?" Haley asked. "Take any of them down?"

"Oh yeah," Malloy answered. "If you guys wanna come out and take a look, we got a few bodies out there. Maybe one of them's the guy that did this to you."

"I doubt we can get that lucky," Recker said. "Any of them escape, that you noticed?"

"A few. I'm sure we'll get them, though, if we go after them. No wonder you guys do so much with so little. The gadgets you guys use are pretty cool."

"Gadgets?"

"The trackers? One of the reasons it took a little longer is Jones wanted to meet up with me before we came down here. He gave me a bunch of trackers to put on any cars we came across here. He said that way if any of them got away, you'd be able to know where they went."

"And did you get them on?" Recker asked.

"Most of them. But the only ones we didn't get are still sitting out there, so we should be good. I'm envious. Now I wish I was in the government so I could get some of those toys."

Recker laughed, though only briefly as it hurt. "We'll sign you up next time."

"Is all that stuff standard issue?"

"Oh yeah. You'd love the laser and stun guns they give you too. And the beam up thing. Out of this world."

Malloy chuckled. "Sounds like it."

They left the room, and went outside, though Recker and Haley were walking a little slower than usual. They were banged up some, though not out of the fight. They didn't think anything was broken, just some bruised ribs, and some cuts on their faces. Nothing that a little time wouldn't cure.

Once they went outside, they saw more of Malloy's men standing around. They were still on high alert in case there was any more activity. But for now, everything was quiet. There were multiple bodies lying around on the pavement, some of them face down.

All told, there were ten bodies on the ground. Recker knew that was a significant chunk of the men that were there. Recker and Haley started walking over to the bodies to see if they could identify any of them.

The ones lying face up were easy. The ones lying face down they turned over. One of them was a surprise. None of them were Petrović. But Max Nilson was among the bodies.

By the way Recker and Haley were standing over the dead body, and looking at each other, Malloy could tell they'd hit on something.

"You know this one?"

"Max Nilson," Recker answered. "One of the leaders of this thing. Maybe the head guy, I don't know. Petrović sure seemed to be deferring to him. There's no doubt about that."

Haley took another glance at all of the faces on the ground. "Unfortunately, Petrović didn't get caught up in all this. Looks like he was one of the lucky ones that got away."

"Only lucky for now," Malloy said. "Like I said, we got trackers planted under the bumpers, just like Jones told us. And the ones that fled, we should have them."

Then a look came over Recker. "We might not even need it."

"Why not?" Haley replied.

"Petrović and Nilson were talking near me. I could hear them. Nilson told him about hurrying up so they could get the ships ready. Then he told Petrović to meet him at the port in three hours. Sounded big."

"That could be what we're waiting for then."

"He could bail on that now," Malloy said. "Especially if you know now."

"Yeah, but they were talking low," Recker replied. "I don't think they knew I was listening. Or cared, to be honest. I don't think they believed I'd be leaving. So Petrović might not even know I heard about the port."

"Doesn't really matter. With those trackers on, even if he decides to bolt and go somewhere else, we'll know it."

"That's assuming he doesn't switch cars or get dropped off somewhere."

"Oh. Yeah."

"Let's hope for the best, though," Haley said.

"We should get going and check in with David," Recker said. He tapped Malloy on the arm. "Thanks for the assist. We'll take it from here."

"Oh no you don't," Malloy replied.

"What?"

"You're not getting rid of us that easy."

"What, you still want in?"

"Damn right. There were still six or seven of them that got away. That still puts you at a disadvantage."

"Who says?" Recker asked.

Malloy smiled. "Who says he doesn't have more men somewhere?"

"That's a good point," Haley answered. "Might not be a bad idea."

"Hey, if you wanna do this, I won't stop you," Recker said.

"We're already involved," Malloy said. "Might as well finish it."

"Plus, it'll help to let people know not to move product around here without Vincent's knowledge and approval, right?"

Malloy smirked and shrugged. "Maybe."

"All right, let's move out," Recker said. "Let's end this thing." He then looked at the two men next to him. "One thing, though. Once we find Petrović, he's all mine. Nobody else takes him out. Make sure everyone else knows that."

"If it gets heated, might not be able to distinguish who's who," Malloy said.

"I understand. But if that's not the case, and there's a chance, I'm the one taking him out."

"Understood."

"He's mine. All mine."

25

Malloy jumped in the backseat of the vehicle with Recker and Haley up front as they sped down the road. They immediately got on the phone with Jones.

"Tell me you're picking something up," Recker said.

"I've got them on my radar, yes," Jones replied.

"Where are they heading?"

"Too soon to tell yet."

"Well what direction?"

"East."

"That doesn't tell me much."

"Well they could be going anywhere," Jones said. "When I know, you'll know. All I can tell you is where the dot is moving. And it's still moving."

They continued driving for about an hour, with Jones relaying what roads he wanted them to take. They were on the right path, but they didn't want to get too close. The last thing they needed to happen was to be spotted. That might ruin everything and cause Petrović to scrap it all and go underground.

But this would probably be their last shot at him. They had to make it count. They had to lay back until it was time to pounce. And then they'd have to smother him so there was no chance of getting up and escaping.

"He's gotta be heading to the port," Recker said.

"He's trending in that direction," Jones replied.

Malloy leaned forward. "Why don't I have a team in place and meet them there?"

Recker quickly shot that down. "No. Because if they can't handle them or keep them in tow before we get there, we could lose them again for good this time."

"Not if they take the same car."

"No guarantee they will, though. We got them right now. No need to rush into anything and spook them."

"He can't be going to a port yet," Haley said.

"Why not?" Recker asked.

"Think about it. His partner, or boss, or whatever their relationship was, Nilson's gone. If that leaves it up to Petrović, and they have multiple warehouses around, he might wanna do a tour first, make sure everything's packed up, everything's being loaded correctly, everything's on the way."

"Unless they've already done all that," Malloy said.

"Well, we were at one of their places earlier today while they were doing it, so there might be some that still haven't packed up yet. And he might want to visit each one to verify with his own eyes."

"Guys, the car's making a turn onto the highway," Jones said. "Looks like they're moving away from the port. At least the Delaware one."

Recker looked at Haley and nodded. "He's got at least one other stop to make."

Recker sped up a little. Not enough to get within striking distance, but closer for when the time came. He didn't want to give Petrović any breathing room.

They drove back over the border into Pennsylvania, and eventually made their way into Delaware County. They knew they hadn't been spotted since they were too far back, but they did wonder if Petrović was aimlessly driving around for a bit, just out of an abundance of caution. They wouldn't have blamed him after what just happened. Thirty more minutes went by until Jones finally had some news to share.

"Guys, it looks like the vehicle has stopped."

"Where?" Recker asked.

"Let me just confirm the address first." Jones typed for a minute, double checking to make sure it was right. "OK. Sending the address to Chris' phone. Looks like it's a warehouse."

Haley looked at his phone, then plugged the address into the GPS.

"Got it," Recker said. "We're about twenty minutes out."

"Plenty of time," Haley replied. "They won't load in that amount of time."

"David, get the schematics of that building."

"I'm already on it," Jones said. "Just keep driving."

As Jones pulled up the map of the building, the others in the car started discussing strategies. It was all preliminary until Jones told them what they were looking at, though. There was no sense in finalizing anything if Jones then told them it wasn't possible based on what he was looking at.

"OK, so here's what we got," Jones said. "I'll send this to Chris' phone too. But it looks like two entrances. One in front, one to the rear. High chain-link fence all around. Medium-sized building."

"How many floors?" Recker asked.

"Just the one, it appears."

"Good."

They hung up, then finalized their plans.

"We'll take the back," Recker said. "Jimmy, you take the front and lead the way up there."

"You want some of my boys back there with you?" Malloy asked.

"How many you got?"

"I got more on the way, should meet us there when we get there."

"Whatever you can spare."

"I'll take ten in the front with me. And I'll send six back there with you."

"Works for me," Recker said.

Once they got to the edge of the building, they dropped Malloy off to be with his men. There were more already waiting to the rear, ready for when Recker and Haley got there. They took a quick look at the front, of which they were a good distance away at the moment. There was a gate which was closed.

"How do you wanna breach?" Malloy asked. "Quiet? Or like a war's starting?"

Recker stared at the gate. "I'm not sure how quiet you can make it. I don't see a guard, but that doesn't mean there isn't one."

"We can drive right through it. Don't matter to me."

Recker nodded. He was good with that strategy.

"How do you wanna coordinate?"

"Give us five minutes to get around to the back and be ready. Then just go. When we hear shooting, that'll be our cue. So start whenever you're ready."

"Sounds good to me."

Malloy tapped the car and backed away as Recker drove away. Once they got to the back of the building, it was a similar situation back there. There was also a locked gate. This was a little different, though. They could see a man standing guard.

Everyone was out of their cars, standing off to the side of the road, protected by the night which blurred their location, and some trees that were nearby.

"Soon as we start, someone nail that guy," Recker said.

"I'll do it," Haley replied.

"Just wait for the signal."

"What signal?"

They then heard a bang, like a car driving through a fence, which was quickly matched by gunfire.

"That one," Recker said.

Haley wasted no time in opening fire, hitting the man by the fence. Recker looked back at one of Malloy's men, who was waiting in a car. Recker motioned for him to go. The man instantly floored it, driving at full speed, going right through the gate and breaking it open.

The rest of the men rushed in. Two men stood by the car and the gate as Recker ordered, just in case any stragglers came out, they wouldn't have a clear escape path. The rest ran toward the back of the warehouse. They found a locked door, but sprayed it with a barrage of bullets, which did the trick and broke it open.

Once inside, they immediately ran down a hallway, checking all rooms they came across. It seemed to be offices, most of which were empty, and a breakroom. They could hear a ton of gunfire going off. By the time they reached the open floor plan, Recker instantly saw the two sides squaring off. To his right was Malloy and his men, shooting across the warehouse at Petrović and his men, who were backpedaling, trying to make it to safety.

There were a ton of pallets and crates throughout the floor, so it wasn't as easy as just opening up and letting it rip. A lot of bullets were being deflected and lodging into the crates. It appeared that Petrović had about ten men with him. There were probably already a couple here by the time Petrović arrived, since he didn't have that many when Recker last saw him, considering the dead bodies.

Recker and his team joined the fight, firing from their direction. Petrović could see he was being squeezed off, and knew they wouldn't be able to hold off for much longer. He had to find an escape path. Recker kept his eyes firmly on Petrović to see what he would do. There was a small window where Petrović was, and he threw something through it to break the glass. He was making his getaway.

Recker knew the situation there was well in hand. He wasn't worried about that. The others would take care of whoever was left. But he wasn't letting Petrović escape again.

Recker ran around a couple of the men he was with, and raced down the hallway to the back door. Once outside, he looked at the men guarding the gate. They were still there.

"Anyone come this way?!"

The men shook their heads. Recker frantically looked around, worried he'd lose his man again. He then ran in the opposite direction to the other side of the building. Once at the corner, he peeked his head around. He didn't see anything at first. Then he closed his eyes and just listened. He heard something. Someone running.

Recker took off in that direction, knowing Petrović must have had something in mind. Running at his top speed, Recker made up some ground, as within a minute, he started to pick up his fleeing adversary. But he had no interest in making this about who had the best 40 time.

He stopped, brought his gun up, carefully aimed, and fired. Petrović went down. Recker quickly ran over to him. By the time he got there, Petrović was getting back to his feet. As well as he could considering he'd been shot in the back of the thigh.

Recker cleared his throat, letting his enemy know he was there. Petrović didn't try moving. He knew that was pointless. With his back still to Recker, Petrović raised his arms. He knew he was defeated. He then slowly turned around to face Recker.

"So what now? You arrest me? Take me to jail? Throw me in a deep, dark hole somewhere?"

"Nope," Recker said.

"Then what?"

"You were right. This was always personal."

Recker then fired at point blank range, hitting Petrović in the chest. His legs instantly gave out as he crashed to the ground. Recker knew it wasn't necessary to check his vitals. He knew what happened to someone who was shot in the chest at that range. But he was taking no chances in Petrović popping back up for a third time a few years down the line. He was making sure that this time the man was really dead. And he was.

By the time Recker stood back up and turned around, he saw Haley approaching him.

"Looks like he's really dead this time."

Recker didn't look happy, but he was finally satisfied with the outcome.

"Yeah. It sure took long enough."

NEXT BOOK

Thank you for reading Execution File. Continue reading The Silencer Series with the next book, Center Mass.

ABOUT THE AUTHOR

Mike Ryan is a USA Today Bestselling Author, and lives in Pennsylvania with his wife, and four children. He's the author of numerous bestselling books. Visit his website at www.mikeryanbooks.com to find out more about his books, and sign up for his newsletter. You can also interact with Mike via Facebook, and Instagram.

 facebook.com/mikeryanauthor
instagram.com/mikeryanauthor

Printed by Amazon Italia Logistica S.r.l.
Torrazza Piemonte (TO), Italy

51499047R00151